CITY LIGHT

Harry Mazer

SCHOLASTIC
HARDCOVER

Scholastic Inc.
New York

Library of Congress Cataloging-in-Publication Data

Mazer, Harry.
City light.

Summary: A teenage boy makes an exploration of his
identity after losing his childhood sweetheart and
beginning a new relationship with the aid of a computer.
[1. Identity—Fiction] I. Title.
PZ7.M47397Ci 1988   [Fic]   87-23486
ISBN 0-590-40511-X

12 11 10 9 8 7 6 5 4 3 2 1   8 9/8 0 1 2 3/9

Printed in the U.S.A.   12

First Scholastic printing, April 1988

For our family and especially for my father, Sam Mazer, and my mother-in-law, Jean Garlen Fox.

Chapter 1

"Is something bothering you, George?" Julie sounded hopeful. She thought I wasn't serious enough about life and the suffering world, all the stuff that filled the news at night. "There's that frown line between your eyes," she said. "Are you thinking about something?" She liked the frown, a sign of a deep thinker thinking deep thoughts.

My mother has the same line between her eyes. It's a family trait. The mark of Farina. The sun is shining, but there's a cloud in the sky, a crease in Farina's eye. I leaned over the counter, raising myself up a little because I'm not that tall, and looked over at her legs in yellow tights. Yellow legs like flower stems.

It was Thursday and she was at work at Buzzy's in the mall. Pumpkin season. Pumpkins and black cats lined the walls, and cutout witches hung from the

1

ceiling. Julie was wearing an orange-and-black uniform and the basic Buzzy beanie.

"What are you doing?" she said.

"Your legs are like tulip stems," I said. Mistake. It wasn't a profound thought. Mere frivolity.

"Seriously," Julie said.

"Seriously?" I said. "I love Julie."

The words sort of hung there, in the air, like one of the cutouts. *I love Julie.* Why did I say it? Julie closed her eyes as if the words really were out there and she didn't want to see them. Julie, you have to understand, was not an excessive person. Julie didn't trust people who talked a lot. Everything about her was spare, a little less than more. She had a narrow, heart-shaped face, small lips, a little point to her chin, a dash for her eyebrows, a dart of a nose. Nothing big or over-flowing about her.

We were almost exactly the same height. Once, I went over to her house in a downpour, got there wet as a rat, and had to change all my clothes. I wore Julie's jeans and one of her shirts. For a while in eighth grade, we'd go out wearing identical outfits. Tan cords and blue shirts or gray cords and green shirts, whatever. We only stopped doing it when Julie said it was getting to be too cutesy.

"Seriously," Julie said again, "you concentrate on us too much, George. There's more to life than us, more to think about than us, us, *us*, all the time."

It was true that *us* was a lot of what I thought about. Us now and us in the future. Julie and George, here in Clifton Heights, Julie with her medical practice and me working for my father or maybe having taken over the business. I could see it. My whole future. My whole life. And I liked it. Was that frivolous? Was that

2

idleness? Didn't thinking about *us* count?

"Order something," Julie said suddenly.

I glanced in the mirror on the column and saw her boss's face, Buzzy himself, wearing the Buzzy beanie and a row of Basic Burger buttons down his jacket. "Pumpkin pie," I said.

"We don't serve pumpkin pie. We've got Basic Burgers, Buzzy's Burger Broil, and Burger Bottoms, a new item on the menu," Julie said, sounding brisk and professional. "A charred, juicy burger on a toasted sesame roll."

"No pumpkin burgers?"

"George, come on," she whispered. "You have to order something."

Friends weren't supposed to hang around during working hours. Buzzy was a dragon about rules. When Julie first got the job, she had to memorize Buzzy's *Code of Conduct*. The little yellow book. Buzzy's own Ten Commandments. Thou shalt smile at all times. Thou shalt be helpful to customers. Thou shalt not conduct personal business while at work. Thou shalt not eat while on duty. Thou shalt not serve your friends. Et cetera.

Question. How can you tell the difference between a boyfriend and a customer? Answer. Customers order. Boyfriends stand around and occupy customer space.

"Big Buzzy soda and Basic Buzzy Burger," I said. Julie got busy filling my order. Her boss disappeared in back. "Hey, Julie," I said, "do I have to pay for this?"

"George, behave!" She slid the food across the counter and held out her hand for the money.

I sat down nearby at a round patio table under an umbrella. There was Julie, hard at work, and here was

3

George, lounging around watching her. Well, I worked, too, for my father, but did that signify? Working for my father was too easy. If I didn't feel like going in, I didn't go in. My father approved when I worked, but he wasn't fanatic about it. If I really didn't want to, I didn't have to. If I said I had homework or something to do at school, he'd let me off. And I still got everything I wanted. More than I asked for. So how tough was that? How real was that?

A father was sitting nearby with his two kids, little girls wearing paper crowns and eating ice cream out of plastic cups. Buzzy came out from the back again, checked Julie, then glanced toward me. I took a big bite of my Basic Burger so he could see I wasn't just taking up space.

Julie had to work. If she wanted anything for herself, if she wanted to go to college, she had to earn the bucks. She worked two days during the week and all day Saturday. On Sundays she volunteered at St. Joseph's Nursing Home, visiting the old people.

"How are you, my man?" I looked up to see my friend Troy with Chris. Ambling by. Troy ambled, Chris bounced. Troy, as always, was as inconspicuous as an Alaskan brown bear.

"How's the wholesome pair?" I pulled out a couple of chairs.

Troy and Chris were wearing sweats and conspicuous sneakers and the red nylon Clifton Heights athletic jackets. Chris played point guard on the girls' varsity basketball team. She was fast and clever on the court, with a nice outside shot, a good arc.

"Waiting for Julie, faithful George?" Chris had a great smile. She was blonde and most people described

4

her as beautiful, but I didn't like to use that word too loosely.

When I thought of someone beautiful, I thought of Julie. Do I sound tiresome? Nobody has to agree with me. Maybe it's corny, but for me, beauty is like a light coming from the inside. Julie had that light. Maybe I was the only one who could see it. That was okay with me. I didn't favor or relish the idea of a lot of guys standing around and talking about Julie's inner light.

Troy sat down. Correction. He didn't sit. He landed. He parked himself. "Sit," he said to Chris, "take a load off your brains." That was supposed to be funny. It went on all the time between them. Me-big-man and you-squaw stuff.

"So what's going on, Georgie?" Troy said. "How long have you been hanging out here?"

"I've lost count. Is it day or night?"

Troy and I have been friends ever since his family crossed the mighty Hudson and landed on the Jersey shore. That was ten years ago, when we were both in second grade. Even then Troy was extra-tall and I was extra-short. We were always a mismatched pair.

He wore baggy jeans and gray sweatshirts that showed his belly and, when he bent over, the elastic waist of his jockey shorts. The only pair of jeans I owned were cutoffs I wore in the summer to wash my father's car. I favored chinos and cotton shirts and sweaters, and loafers.

I was particular about the clothes I wore and how I wore them. Clothes made me feel good, they made me feel complete and whole, aware of limits, aware of where I ended and the world began. I got the feeling sometimes that I was a neatly wrapped package, all the

5

strings tied, the address label and stamps in place. It gave me a good, secure feeling about myself, like I was all there and in control. What you see is what I am.

Troy was an outlaw, an anarchist; he didn't believe in rules. He believed in freedom. He could have been a communist for all I knew. He went to school, but he considered it a waste of time. He played football, but he thought all the hoopla was pathetic. Coach Burmeister was always threatening to throw him off the team, but Troy on the line was formidable.

He never studied, but he got by without any trouble. He more than got by. He knew a hell of a lot. It was from reading books all the time. He had a book stuffed in his back pocket now.

"What are you eating?" he said.

"Buzzy's Basic Burger."

He sniffed it, picked it up, and finished it off in one bite. "More."

I pointed to Buzzy's.

"How much dollaroso?"

I pulled out all I had with me, a buck, and laid it on the table.

"What will that get us?" Troy said. "Chris? You got any money? You're always hungry."

"You just ate a whole pizza."

"You see, you can't trust a woman to keep a confidence." He handed her the dollar. "Woman, get me three of those burgers."

"You're crazy. He's crazy, George. A dollar will buy you one, great man." She went up to the counter.

"So is this what you do all the time?" Troy said, turning to me. "What are you, afraid to let her out of your sight?"

6

"Don't you have football practice? What are you doing here, anyway?"

"I skipped out early. I got hungry."

"What'd you tell the coach?"

"Nothing." He glanced up at Chris, who had just come back. "Sit down," he said. "You're not waiting on tables."

Chris kicked his foot. "Don't tell me stupid things."

"I'll tell you as many stupid things as I want to tell you."

"No, you won't!"

I looked from one to the other. Were they serious? A moment ago they were laughing, everything was funny, and now they were staring each other down, looking grim as gargoyles.

"Arm wrestle?" I said to break the tension. I set my elbow on the table. Overall, Troy beats me more times than I beat him, but I can hold him pretty good, because I put more into it.

Troy winked at Chris. "You root for me."

"Why should I?" She took a bite of the burger.

" 'Cause you're my woman." He rubbed her back with his free hand and I took him.

He took me the next three times.

"My turn," Chris said.

"You never win," Troy said.

"I don't want to wrestle you."

"I'll go left-handed with you, Chris," I said.

"Because I'm a girl? No thanks, George. All or nothing."

"Prepare to lose." I got set. I knew Chris had a good grip, but I looked over to see if Julie was watching and lost my concentration. Chris beat me with a single, quick, hard move.

7

"Take her on left-handed," Troy jeered.

"Don't rub it in," Chris said. "George did his mighty best."

They both laughed. Whatever their fight had been about, it was over as quickly and mysteriously as it had started. They were friends again and left holding hands.

Julie quit work early. She was having cramps and the smell of food was making her feel really sick.

We walked along the dark streets, cars on one side, hedges on the other. It was uphill most of the way from Bergen Boulevard. "How do you feel now?" I asked. "Cramps any better?"

"A little. Not much. . . ."

It's always difficult to know what to say to someone who isn't feeling good. The truth is, you don't *really* feel someone else's pain. I cared because it was Julie and she was hurting, but the main thing was, I wanted her to know I knew she felt lousy. And that was a little phony.

"George, is your father going to sell our house?"

Julie's family lived in an apartment house that my father owned. It sat on the cliffs overlooking the Hudson and had a great view of the New York skyline. The developers had their eye on it. They'd already bought the property on either side.

"My parents are worried," Julie said. "They say Muggleston needs the land our house is on to put up his condos. It's money, George. Why are you shaking your head? He'll pay anything to get property along the cliffs."

"My father wouldn't do it, Julie. He's not going to put you out. He doesn't want those condos in Clifton Heights. You know what he told me once? He'd like to keep one of the apartments in your house for him-

8

self, so he could go over there anytime he wants to and look out over the river."

"He wants to live in our house?"

"I don't know if he'd really do it, but he talks about it sometimes. He's just like your father about that view. You know how he feels about this town. He wants it to stay a small town. He doesn't want a lot of new people and traffic coming in. He won't sell. He'll never sell."

She shrugged. What did that mean? Didn't she believe me? Was she resentful because my father had the power to put them out of their house? Or was something else wrong? She'd been so cool all afternoon. I thought it, then I dismissed the thought. Nothing was wrong, Julie just didn't feel good.

At her door, we kissed. She touched her lips to mine. I held her, but she slid away and went in. The door clicked shut.

As soon as she was gone, I felt lonely for her. I crossed the street and looked up at the lit windows, hoping to catch a glimpse of her.

Chapter 2

GEORGE LOVES JULIE FOREVER AND EVER AND EVER.

Maybe you've seen that sign on one of the pedestrian walkways that snake around and over the Jersey side of the George Washington Bridge. I did it a couple years ago after Julie and I had a big fight. We broke up for several days, almost a whole week. I don't remember what the fight was about. I only remember how I felt. Like I was bleeding and dying. Like I had to do something drastic, excessive, to get her back.

GEORGE LOVES JULIE FOREVER AND EVER AND EVER.

In red, crudely formed letters. Almost childish, kindergarten letters. Not exactly George Washington's script. His woman's name was Martha. This was George Farina's hand. Not the father of his country, more like a thief, scanning the crumbling stairs, a broad, felt-tipped magic marker in his fist, the light coming down on him through the protective mesh screening put there to protect walkers from bottle-heaving travelers.

If you were riding by in your car on your way out of the city, you could have seen all this. Seen me. Sicko, you would have thought, sicko kid writing on the wall. Exhibitionist Jersey hood. Pimply adolescent.

Had you unexpectedly come upon me on the stairs, maybe you'd have turned and gone the other way. Yeah, you would have if you'd seen my face, seen the red squiggly lines down my cheeks and across my forehead. Decorated like a birthday cake. He's a loony, you'd have thought, and jumped back, the blood sinking in your stomach. And if you had the guts to go past me, you'd have held yourself as far from me as you could, as if I were a disease you didn't want to catch.

That time, when we made up, I took Julie to see my artwork. "You did that, George?"

Was she impressed? If she'd done something like that for me, I'd be impressed. I'd be kicking up my heels, turning cartwheels. But even when Julie was impressed, she was impressed quietly. Everyone says opposites attract. It was true about me and Julie. And Troy and me. Even my parents. Real opposites.

My father was a hugger. He couldn't come near anybody without putting his arm around them. My mother had plenty of affection, but she was a lot crisper with people. She didn't even hug my sister and me that much.

My parents worked together in my father's shop, worked together every day, but they didn't agree on a thing. Not even their cars. My mom drove a VW convertible, old but in great shape. My father hated

11

it. She loved it. She used to buzz around in a VW before she was married. "It makes me feel young," she said. My father drove a Cadillac Seville. He was a little bit of a big shot — not that he was obnoxious about it — but he liked nice stuff, great clothes, and big cars. He had a diamond on his pinky. "Why not, I work for it," he said.

He wanted my mother to drive a bigger car. "That Bug isn't safe," he said, which was half true. Mom admitted that when she drove the Bug, big cars were always taking advantage. "Especially at intersections, when I have the right of way. Then you can count on it, some bully of a car is going to try to jump out in front of me."

Sometimes I felt like life was like that, like a road packed with cars and trucks. Troy was one of the trucks, big enough that he didn't have to worry who was in his way. Julie was more like a Mercedes or a BMW — quality stuff, safe, not needing to throw her weight around to prove anything. Me, I was like that VW Bug of Mom's. Whatever you were, though, you had to be quick to stay in the fast lane. I didn't care if I was in the fast lane or not, but when you were a bug you had to be alert just to keep from being crushed.

Once I told Julie my theory of Life Is a Road. "That sounds so negative," she said. "Do you think of yourself as a bug?"

"I do not."

"As something about to be crushed underfoot?"

"No, Julie, that's not the point."

"George, are you sorry you're short?"

"Are you kidding? It's better to be short."

"Good. That sounds more positive."

"Short people live longer. Their bodies are more

12

efficient — less distance for blood to travel."

"Doesn't sound too scientific," Julie said doubtfully.

"Take my word for it. Tall men go soft and get potbellies and their hair falls out. Short men are wiry and sexy and women can't keep their hands off them."

"Tell me about it," Julie said.

"Short people have better posture, too. Less to hold up straight. Short people are closer to the ground, which means they're more practical, they don't have their heads in the clouds. I could go on, but I think I've made my point."

"You mean there's more?"

"Julie! What about wrestling?"

"What about it?"

"You've seen me. Short is good in wrestling, too. When I'm on the mat, I can always tell when my opponent is measuring himself against me, flexing his long arms and legs, and imagining how he's going to tie this short guy up in knots."

"And?"

"And I go right through those big guys, don't I? I get under them, go for their hips and lift them off the ground. Then what can they do? Then they're the bugs spinning around on their backs. Now, what do you say?"

"Do I have any choice?" She raised her hands. "Okay, okay, short is better, George. Short is much better."

I was twelve when I met Julie. I had gone to her house that day with my father. He was there to collect the rent. I was there to be with him. While he went upstairs, I stood outside, looking over the edge of the cliff, down at the river and across to New York City. It was like looking out of the real world into something bright and mysterious.

13

We didn't go over to the city much. "Here, it's better," my father said. He didn't have anything good to say about New York. Here, he said, we knew the streets, we knew our neighbors, we knew the names of all the dogs who came out to greet us. My grandfather had moved here from Brooklyn when my father was a little boy. My grandfather had had a barber shop on Bridge Street. It was a laundromat now.

My mother had lived in Clifton Heights all her life. And so had I. All my life, I'd looked across to New York City. I suppose if I thought about New York City at all, what I thought was that it was over there and I was over here and that was the way I liked it.

Standing there that day, I noticed a path and steps leading down the cliff. Had there been steps across the water, I wouldn't have taken them, but down the face of the cliff was something else. That was interesting.

I started down. I'd only gone a few steps when something hit me in the back. *Ping!* I took another step, and I got a stinger in the neck. Another step and I was hit again. *Ping! Ping!* Something small and white rolled down the steps. I picked it up. A miniature marshmallow. I was hit again.

"Hey!" I yelled.

Above me I noticed a thicket of bushes, actually a tree with its top lopped off and boards hammered down to make a platform. I saw a foot; a sneaker; a skinny, bare, scratched-up leg. I sprang for the tree and scrambled up to the edge of the platform.

"Stop!" a girl said.

"Hi," I said. It was Julie.

She looked down at me. "This is private property. You're trespassing."

"You attacked me."

14

"I did not." She had a bag of marshmallows in her hand.

"Where did those come from?"

She looked down as if she'd never noticed them before. "You're trespassing," she said again.

"You're the one who's trespassing," I said. "I own this place."

"You? Who are you?"

"George Farina. My father owns this land and apartment house."

"That means you're trespassing, too," she said. "You don't own it, either."

Her logic escaped me. "I'm coming up." I said and climbed up. "Did you build it?" I asked.

She nodded. "It won't hold you."

I bounced up and down. "Solid," I said and sat down. It was a neat place. Sitting there was like being suspended in the air, hanging over the cliff and the river.

She kept looking at me. I couldn't tell if she liked me or not. I already knew I liked her.

When I heard my father calling, I didn't want to go. I heard him overhead, at the edge of the cliff. I didn't want him to know about the platform. I put my finger to my lips and smiled at Julie. "I'll be back," I said.

I went back the next day, came over on my bike. Julie was on the platform, reading. "Oh. Hi," she said.

"Can I come up?"

"Okay."

We talked for a long time. She said she came there to read or just watch the birds. There were birds everywhere in the thickets and wild grapevines growing down the cliffs. Julie had trained a robin to come to her hand for food. That's what the marshmallows were for. She told me if I was quiet, the robin would come back. And it did. It landed on her shoulder. It had a dark head and a yellow eye. It hopped down on her open hand and snagged a marshmallow. Julie's face was glowing.

I think that was the exact moment I fell in love with Julie. It didn't matter that I was just a kid. It didn't matter that I was only twelve years old. I fell in love with her as hard as anybody could fall in love, and I knew right then that I'd never love anybody else the way I loved Julie.

Chapter 3

"Here at last, my prince," my mother said when I walked into my father's shop. Mom was behind the reception desk, wearing a gray silk dress with a string of pearls, and her hair short and smooth. She took care of the business end of things, made sure that everyone who worked was in on time, the appointments ran smoothly, and the customers were taken care of. She gave me a kiss. "Daddy's waiting for you," she whispered.

In grade school, I used to get into fights all the time over my father's business. Chuck Langione or Dick Bielick would come along and say, "Hey, Farina! Your father runs a beauty parlor."

"You got it wrong," I'd say. "It's an ugly parlor. They got a special on today for guys like you. You want to get your mug fixed?"

17

"Hey, Farina! Let me see your hands. You got a manicure?"

"Not as good as yours, Bielick. Where do you get your nails done? A horse barn?"

"Hey, Farina! Your father does ladies' hair!"

"You want to make an appointment? What do you want done? Shampoo? Set? Facial massage? Pull the hairs out of your ears?"

"You wouldn't catch me in a place like that."

"Don't worry, Bielick, you couldn't get in. They don't cut apes' hair."

About that time Dick's eyes would be nearly squinted shut and his hands would be making fists. He was bigger than me, but then so was every boy in the class, except Arthur Stone. Dick started the pushing. I said he had a face that belonged in a sack of potatoes. He shoved me. I shoved him back. It was a short fight. He held me off with one hand and popped me in the nose with the other. A couple of pops and my nose was producing tomato juice.

"Had enough?" he said.

"Not till I pull you apart."

Another pop in the nose.

"Quit?"

I wiped the blood from my nose and smeared it on his shirt.

"Hey! My shirt! You ruined my shirt."

"That's just a sample of what you're going to get."
I kicked him in the leg and ran. Then I had to stay out of his way for the rest of the week.

Leonard was my father's name and the name of his business. Just Leonard's. Not Leonard's Beauty Salon. Not Leonard's Hair Stylists. Not Leonard's Sheer Magic. Just the one word. Leonard's. More class. Leonard's wasn't one of those little storefront places you saw strung along every block. There were as many beauty parlors in Clifton Heights as there were grocery stores.

A long time ago, before my sister, Joanne, was born, my father had a storefront place, too, on Anderson Avenue, but around the time I was four years old, my parents bought an old brick firehouse near Bergen Boulevard and renovated it. They put big windows in front and a spiral staircase going up to the second floor to the Beauty and Relaxation Room. There were paintings on the walls and statues of winged cherubs, hanging plants and intersecting windows, and a waiting room with comfortable chairs and magazines. The coffeepot was always on.

Outside, a flagpole flew the LEONARD's banner: yellow letters on a purple background, the royal purple. We shared a parking lot with the Pickwick Club, where they had tennis and squash courts. They get a pretty tony trade there, and my father gets the benefit of it. A lot of men, especially, go in to play tennis and then come over to Leonard's to have a shampoo or a haircut.

Near the register, where my mother worked, there was a row of celebrity pictures showing my father shaking hands with the mayor of Clifton Heights or with the police chief. He's even got one of him shaking hands with the pride of New Jersey, The Boss, Bruce Springsteen. You might think that was the one I liked best, but the picture I got the biggest kick out of showed my father, all five feet four of him, reaching up to shake hands with the Jets' wide receiver Eli Green, all six feet five of *him*.

My father was at work. He had the first chair, behind the half-wall separating the reception area from where the work goes on. My father wore glasses at work. He

19

was round-faced, sort of grim-looking, except when he smiled. Then his whole face broke open. When he smiled, it was like a jailbreak. "Is that my son?" he said.

"Yeah, Pop, it's me."

"My son is here," he announced. My father is loud and proud. Everyone in Leonard's heard him and maybe over at the Pickwick Club, too.

His cubicle was a little bigger than anyone else's, but that was the only sign he was the boss. He didn't swing his weight around. The closest he got to that was when he lectured the new stylists. "Hairdressing is an art." (I knew his spiel by heart. I'd heard it often enough.) "Barbers cut grass. Chop, chop. The grass gets long, they run a machine over it. Chop, chop. That's not what we do here. Hair expresses something about a person. Look at the whole person, not just the hair. The personality, that's the art of it."

He was combing out Mrs. Ellison, a regular customer. I watched him work for a few minutes. "How'd you like to have a head of hair like that," he said, pulling me over. "Isn't that a beautiful head of hair?"

Lucy went by and pulled my ear. She was wearing a pink smock, her glasses around her neck on a chain. "You're late," she said. Lucy's been with my father for years.

I went downstairs into the storeroom and began cleaning up, stacking supplies, sweeping, throwing out empty boxes. I had the radio on. Lucy came halfway down the stairs to tell me to bring up several bottles of shampoo.

Back downstairs again, I was arranging bottles on a shelf, when my father came in. He lit a cigarette and sat down on a box. "My feet hurt."

"You're carrying too much weight, Pop. You need to get in shape."

His hand went to his belly. "Short and fat, that's your father. What's wrong with being short and fat?" He exhaled a stream of smoke toward the ceiling. "Short, fat, and I like cigarettes, too. Don't tell me what they're going to do to me. It seems that the older I get the less I'm allowed to do. All my pleasures turn into poisons."

"Doesn't have to be that way."

"You're right, but I don't think I'm going to change now. . . . George, what are you going to do when your father can't?"

"Can't what, Pop?"

"Can't. Just can't. Can't snip, can't cut hair, can't lift a pair of scissors. I'm out of shape, cigarette-poisoned. You listening, son? What then? What are you going to do with your life?"

"With my life?" I hated that expression. It always made me uneasy. My life was fine. I didn't want to do anything with it. I liked it the way it was. I was with Julie. I had my friends. Someday, probably, I'd go to work with my father the way he had with his father. But I didn't want to say it, because I didn't want to do it now. Maybe I wanted to try some other things first. The one thing I was totally sure about was Julie. I'd once made the mistake of telling that to my parents.

"Okay, you're certain about her and we'll assume she's certain about you," my mother had said, "at least for the present moment." And here she gave me a look that said, You're a nice boy, but you've still got a lot to learn. "And what are you offering Julie?" she'd said.

21

"Me," I'd said. Another indulgent look from my mother.

My father looked at me like I had a leak in my head. "George, George, you're going to have to do better than that. You're going to have to earn, you're going to have to provide."

I can't remember who said what. It was a chorus. They took turns. "George, you're going to be a man, you have to have a steady income. Where's it going to come from?"

"You don't have to worry about me," I told them. "I'm thinking about things." Not true, but it was my only defense. And now I said, "You don't have to worry, Pop. I won't let you go to the poorhouse on foot."

"No, you'll drive me there in your Cadillac."

"Understood." It was an old joke between us.

"Now you know you can always come in here in the business. Don't look like I just gave you a bellyache. I started with my father, didn't I? I didn't do so bad. You've got a feeling for it, too. You've got the eye. You just need a little training. There's a lot worse things that you could do."

"Right, Dad, I could be a pick-and-shovel man." I'd heard the lots-worse-things speech before, too. In the back of my mind, I agreed with my father. The business was there and it made me feel safe, though I'd never admit it. One of these days I'd step in, but right now I didn't want to think about it.

"All my customers know you already. When your mother and I are ready to retire, they'll just keep right on with you. They'll come for you, too. They'll bring their friends and their kids here. They all like you. George, they say, he's such a nice boy. And I say, right, not like his father. I tease them, but they really mean it. They like you, son. You've got the personality. This business is about two things. One is knowing your job, how to make the most of hair, whatever it is you're doing, cutting or styling or coloring, and the other is customers. That's the bottom line, George. If you have a loyal clientele and you treat them right, you'll live a comfortable life."

He finished his cigarette and got up. "My appointment is waiting. Think about what I said."

"Okay."

"The time is coming when you have to make a decision."

"I know, Pop."

"You're going to think about it?"

I nodded, but what I was thinking about was calling Julie. We hadn't made our plans for tonight yet.

"You want to help me with Fitzy today?"

"Mrs. Fitzgerald? Her again?"

"She's not so bad."

"She's never satisfied. If you do her today, she'll be in tomorrow to complain."

"She never goes anywhere else. She's a good customer."

"If you say so, Pop."

When I was done in the supply room, I went out to see what else anyone wanted me to do.

"I'm set," Paul said. He was doing a coloring job, rolling in the Saran Wrap. His client was really beautiful. I wondered why she wanted to change her hair color. Maybe she just wanted Paul to work on it. Paul's got dozens of women crazy over him. He's handsome, dresses like a prep, looks like he's straight out of Princeton. He's worked at Leonard's for about five years.

"Sweep me up, lover," Inez said. She's tall, every week has a different hairstyle, every month a different color. This month she was a redhead. She had a new perm.

"Looks good," I said, sweeping up the hair.

"You like it? I'm not so sure." She was cutting a customer I didn't recognize. Inez had long, clever fingers that fascinated me. Watching her cut hair was like watching Troy at the piano. Their fingers had a life of their own. "George, did you hear about the superjock who got straight A's but still wasn't happy?"

"Is this serious?" her customer asked. He had a small head; his hair was thin on top and long in back.

Inez put her hand on his shoulder. "If you laugh, it's a joke." She went back to cutting his hair, lifting it strand by strand. "So, this guy, I'm telling you he was a superjock, he was a basketball player, he was great on the court, plus he made straight A's."

"So what was his problem?" I said. I always played straight man for Inez. "Why was he so unhappy?"

" 'Cause his B's were still a little bit crooked."

I groaned, and the guy in the chair turned to look up at Inez. She handed him a mirror and whirled the chair around so he could see the back of his head. "You don't think that's funny?" she asked. "Dumb jock joke. Better than those dumb Polack jokes you hear. I'm Polish. I don't like those jokes."

"Nice haircut," he said.

She took off the smock and brushed his shoulders. He was wearing a vest. He gave her a fifty-cent tip and left.

"Twenty-two bucks for the haircut," Inez said, "and he can't afford a dollar tip." She pocketed the coin. "What are you doing today, George?"

24

"I'm going to see Julie."

"Uh-huh. Well, what else is new? Oh, I gotta have a smoke before my next customer." She took off for the bathroom.

When I had a moment, I called Julie's house. Beth, her older sister, answered the phone. "Hello, Beth," I said. "This is George. Is Julie there?"

"George?" she said. "George who?"

A simple telephone call with Beth was like a sparring match. "George," I said, "as in Julie and George."

"George Crispin?"

"Who's he?"

"Who's this?"

"Okay, Beth, this is George *Farina*."

"Spell that, will you?"

"Sure, Beth. You've only known me for six years, I don't expect you to remember my name. Are you ready? This is *space* G-E-O-R-G-E *space* F-A-R-I-N-A. Can I *space* T-A-L-K *space* to *space* J-U-L-I-E?"

"Oh, George! My friend, George Farina! Why didn't you say so?"

"Love your sense of humor, Beth."

"It's not bad," she said modestly. "Wait a minute, George Farina." When she came back, she said, "Uh, George? Uh . . . Julie doesn't want to talk to you right now."

"What's she doing?"

"Who knows with Julie? She's got her head in a book."

"Did you tell her it was me?"

"I think so."

"Tell her again."

"Sure, George, anything for you. . . . Julie . . . Julie! George is on the phone. . . ." A moment later,

25

she was back to me. "George? She said she didn't feel like talking right now. But Mom says for you to come over for supper."

"Is Julie okay?"

"I guess so, George. See you later. Pick up a loaf of bread on the way over. Italian bread."

"Understood." I hung up.

Chapter 4

Julie's father took another serving of lasagna and passed the dish to me. "Thanks, Mr. Walsh." He had his cuffs rolled back so you could see the blue snake tattooed around his wrist, the head on the inside curling toward his palm.

"Is it good, George?" Beth said.

"Why do you ask him?" Julie said. "He'll eat anything. Ask me."

Beth had made supper. She was four years older than Julie and completely different. Beth never stopped joking, and she was totally uninterested in school. ("I was lucky to get out of high school alive.") She worked nights at Sperry Products as a packer.

"It's really good, Bethy," Julie's mother said.

"You should see the timbers we pulled out of that building today." Mr. Walsh held out his arms. "Twenty-four inches across." He did demolition work in the city. There was a picture of him in the hall showing him standing high in an empty window on the side of a building, wearing his safety hat and goggles and holding a wrecking bar. He tore down buildings during the day, and at night he'd sit in his reclining chair and read history.

Julie was proud of her father, but, for no reason I could ever understand, she was always arguing with her mother. I liked both Julie's parents. Her mother was friendly, relaxed, an unpretentious person. Mrs. Walsh worked in a sports club, and Julie and I used her free court time a lot.

"They put a new man on the clam," Mr. Walsh was saying, "and I had to snake timbers around all day."

I liked hearing Mr. Walsh talk about his work. I sometimes thought about apprenticing myself to him. We'd go to work together every day in our jeans and work boots, carrying lunch pails. I'd work hard, develop my muscles, sweat a lot. I'd shower every day when I got home. Julie and I would be married, and I'd want to smell good for her. We could live with her parents at first.

I touched shoulders with Julie. Did she know what I was thinking? I leaned against her, but she didn't press back. I didn't think anything of it then, just went on fantasizing about being married to her, living with her family. We all got along. We'd gone places together lots of times. Sundays, when my father liked to relax at home with music and his shoes off, Julie's dad liked to drive around, usually over to the city.

We never drove through the Lincoln Tunnel without my thinking it was going to spring a leak, so I was always glad when Mr. Walsh drove over to the city

28

on the G. W. Bridge. That way, you saw the river down below, the skyline of the city, and the bridge itself, cables against the blue sky, like a skeleton, every bone and sinew in perfect tension and harmony.

In the city Mr. Walsh would take the West Side Highway downtown. Julie and I would always try to spot their house on the other side of the river. Sometimes we'd go over to the Museum of Natural History. Or we'd walk around the park. People everywhere on the grass and rocks. It was like going to the shore. Wall-to-wall bodies. And watch your step! Dogs and dog droppings. I never got that excited about New York.

Julie, though, loved the city. She was always discovering things. I remember one day in the park, she found a wooden pavilion way up on some high rocks. Her parents didn't want to make the climb, so the two of us scrambled up and sat in the pavilion with the sun in our faces and talked about the kind of house we'd live in someday.

"Julie." Her mother looked at her watch. "I have to go to work." She had on a tan jogging suit with the logo of the club on the pocket. "Do you mind cleaning up tonight?"

Julie was up like a shot. "I'm gone," she said, and she left.

"You'll help her, won't you, George?"

"Understood."

Mrs. Walsh passed me the bread basket. "What colleges are you applying to, George?"

"I haven't decided."

"Are you applying to the same schools as Julie? I think it would be nice if you kids end up in the same school."

"Why?" Julie said.

"The first year of college is hard, honey. It'll help if you know someone."

"Don't you think I can make friends?"

"What are you getting upset about? Of course I do."

"You don't sound like it. You sound like you think I need George as my nursemaid."

"That's not what I meant, Julie."

"No?"

"All right, you two," Julie's father said. "I want a peaceful supper. Mary, how's your knee?"

"It bothered me when I ran." She glanced over at Julie, who was frowning down at her plate.

"You told me you weren't going to run every day."

"I couldn't help myself," Mrs. Walsh said. "I feel like such a slug if I don't do something." She touched Julie's hand. "I don't want us to be fighting, honey. I just want you to be smart and happy. You and George — "

"Mom!" Julie's face was on fire. "Stop deciding my life for me."

There was a tense silence. Then Julie's mother sighed. "Let's talk about something else. Apple pie and French vanilla ice cream for dessert. I know George is one taker. Who else? Chuck?"

"When did I ever pass up dessert?"

"Julie?"

"No, thanks." She got up and started clearing the dishes.

Later, while Julie and I were doing the dishes, she got going on her mother. "She acts like she knows my future. Mary and her crystal ball. Go to the same college George is going to. Where does she get that stuff?" She dipped a glass in the sudsy water. "She

30

doesn't know where I'm going, she doesn't know what I'm going to do. What if I don't even want to go to college?"

"Don't you?" I put a dish away in the cupboard.

"Of course I do. You know I'm premed. But what if I change my mind? Maybe I'll go into something else. Something I haven't even thought of yet. Maybe I'll be an actress! My mother thinks my life is going to be just like hers. A little bit of school, then get married *to George*, have kids, bring them up, get a job, go from one day to another day, mess around in my kids' lives the way she does. God!"

"Julie. Your mom just wants things to be good for you."

"Great! And I just want to strangle her. But I'm going to do what I want to do, no matter what she says." Julie looked over at me and smiled, faintly. "Right?"

"You know, you could talk to her a little bit more, though, the way you do to your father."

"The voice of reason," Julie said.

"Well. . . ."

She sighed and leaned against me for a moment. "No, you're right. You're a nicer person than I am, George."

"No way."

"Yes, you are," she insisted. "You don't fight with your parents. You're loyal, you're not like me."

There was something about the way she was looking at me that scared me. She said I was one way and she was another, that we were somehow divided. Dividable. And a moment later, she said it.

"You know," she said. "I'm sure you know. . . . George, we're not going to be together forever."

31

People always said things like that. You're young. Things change. Things aren't going to stay the way they are. I heard the words, I knew what they meant, but I didn't want to hear it.

I pulled Julie around and looked at her face. I held her tightly and thought, I must have kissed those lips ten thousand times. And I knew that I could kiss them ten thousand more times and never get tired of it.

The first time we ever kissed was on the cliff. We were thirteen years old. It was *our* place by then, not just Julie's. Below the platform, we'd found a level spot where we were making a garden. That day we'd slid down to the garden and were working on chopping steps into the slope up to the platform.

It was a hot day. No wind. I had my shirt off. Julie's face was shiny with heat. She had her shirt tied up in front. Sweat was running down my face and my neck. "Oh, are you wet," Julie said.

"How about you?"

"Whew." She fanned her face and sat down with her back against the cliff. "I'm sweaty, too."

I sat down next to her. We looked at each other and kissed. Then we looked out over the river. A hot wind stirred the leaves around us. Far below there was the hum of traffic and machines, and the river like a leaden, silent snake.

Our lips touched again.

"George," she said. "What does it make you feel like?"

I wiped Julie's face with my T-shirt. Then I wiped her neck and under her shirt. "Why don't you take that off?" I said. My voice stuck in my throat.

"Take off my shirt?"

"You have a bra on." She took off her shirt. She

32

was wearing a white bra. We kissed again, wet, salty kisses. My lips slid around her mouth. I put my hands on her bare shoulders. I was surprised how bony they were.

"No hands," Julie said and we put our hands behind our backs. For the rest of the summer, that was the way we kissed — without shirts and no hands.

For a long time, the cliff was the only place we kissed. Sometimes we'd kiss for what seemed like hours, kissed and talked. We felt we were extraordinarily mature. We were handling things. Sex wasn't taking us over.

"We could be friends and not kiss," Julie said one day.

"No, that wouldn't be as good."

She agreed. "We can do both, be friends and kiss. And we'll tell each other things about how we feel. It'll be like a science course."

"All right, students," I said, "our lesson today is sex. What is the purpose of sex? Why is there sex? Why do we have male and female? Julie Walsh, you have your hand raised. Why do we have male and female?"

"So we can have kissing."

"Correct!"

By the end of the next summer, when we kissed, Julie was taking off her bra. This is the way it happened. One day, she said, "Wait." She turned her back and unsnapped the bra. I watched her, my eyes fixed on the slope of her shoulders, her elbows jutting out, her shoulder blades outlined against her back. She turned around. "What do you think?"

There was her face. And there were her breasts. I couldn't speak. I had seen breasts in magazines, but this was the first time I'd seen the real thing on a real girl. And it wasn't any girl, it was Julie.

Kissing her like that was hypnotic. The feeling was so thick and intense it made me dizzy. We were close, closer than we'd ever been, but I wanted to be closer. Wanted to slide down on the ground with her. Wanted more.

My pants were stained when we stopped. She noticed. She said, "Let's never do this again." But her cheeks were shining and her lips were shining like red candies. "We're not going to do anything dumb. Are we, George?" Her eyes were large, bright, as if there were a light shining from behind them, a light fixed on me, searching my face and my mind and reaching into my heart.

It was that look, that shining light in Julie's eyes, that kept me from doing "anything dumb." We could wait. *I* could wait. I could wait for as long as I had to for Julie, and I wouldn't love her any less or any more for waiting.

"You know what I'm thinking about?" I said now, standing in her kitchen, my lips against her hair. "I'm thinking about the first time we kissed."

"Oh, that."

"You think we'll ever forget it?"

"We were just dumb kids."

"Not so dumb. We knew something about us, something we still know."

She moved away from me and felt around in the water for another dish. "George, we're not twelve years old anymore."

"There are some things that never change," I said. "You and I are never going to change."

"Oh, George, do you really believe that? How can

34

you? Everything changes." She was facing the window, not looking at me, peering out into the dark.

I kissed her neck.

"Not now," she said.

"Yes, now." I pulled her against me, kissed her until she kissed me back and her cheeks were shining and red the way they'd been the first time we kissed.

Chapter 5

"You should have heard Marsha Feldman today in the cafeteria," my sister said.

I had my head in the freezer, trying to decide between macaroni and cheese, or chicken pie.

"She started on me, 'You know, Joanne, you think you're so clever all the time.' "

"Uh-huh," I said. Maybe chicken pie. Last night had been macaroni. Most nights, supper came straight from the freezer into the microwave. By the time my mother got home, all she wanted to do was grab a tray and collapse in front of the TV.

"And so I said to her, 'Look, Marsha, you call yourself my friend — ' "

"Uh-huh, uh-huh," I said. On the other hand, chicken pie was so boring.

36

Joanne punched me in the back. "Hey!" I turned around. To look at my sister, you'd think her bones were made of water, but she packed a good punch. "What was that for?" I said.

"For not listening. '*Uh-huh, uh-huh, uh-huh.*' " She was wearing pink tights and green shorts, had her hair in pigtails. "You can't fool me, George. You weren't listening."

"Very good, very good," I said. "Attack, attack. That's the first rule of a good defense. Strike the first blow." I've been teaching Joanne the basics of self-defense. She's twelve years old and twice as smart as anybody in our family, but she doesn't use her body enough. She spends too much time reading and sitting in front of her computer.

"You know, George, you *don't* listen when I'm talking."

"Joanne, I was thinking about what I'm going to eat — "

"No, you don't pay attention, you don't care how I feel."

"Don't be so sensitive, Joanne."

"I'll stop being sensitive when you stop being dense."

I danced around her on my toes, shadow-boxing. "In the ring, ladies and gentlemen, in the khaki chinos, we have Tricky Dense. And in the pink tights, So Sensitive, two able opponents. This is a fifteen-round championship fight. No punching below the belt, no clinching, no hanging on, and may the best hu-man win." I thought that would get a smile out of Joanne, but she stood there, frowning at the floor.

"You know, today I had two different-colored ribbons in my hair, and Marsha said it was too cute for words. Why does she say things like that?"

37

"Probably jealous. Isn't her hair short?"

"It's cute, very cute. I'm stuck with these dopey braids." She grabbed a braid and made snipping motions.

"Mom doesn't want you to cut your hair."

"I think that's ridiculous. It's my hair."

I decided on the macaroni, after all, and put it into the microwave. "You going to eat?"

"I'm not thinking about food right now. I have other things on my mind."

"Uh-huh."

"There you go again! You don't know anything about women, do you, George?"

"I didn't know we were talking about women."

"Hilarious!" She walked out.

"Don't go away mad," I called after her. She didn't answer. I took the macaroni out of the microwave, poured soda into two glasses, got a couple of forks and napkins, put it all on a tray, and brought it up to Joanne's room.

She was in front of her computer. "Go away."

"Peace. I bring food. And a fork so you can share my macaroni."

"Okay, in a minute."

I sat down on her bed and ate and watched her. Joanne had had a PC since she was nine years old and it became clear to Mom and Dad that she and computers had a special relationship. My sister was one of those computer whiz kids. She was never far from that machine. I didn't have any doubt that computers were in her future. Anything in our house that was electronic and beeped and burped and sometimes talked back belonged to my sister. She was probably a genius, and it was either going to make her rich someday or

38

get her locked up. My hunch was she'd make a million before she was thirty.

For Joanne's birthday a few weeks before, Mom and Dad had updated her computer and bought her a modem. She had figured out how to use it in a few hours, and overnight got herself a computer pal in California, a kid named Kevin. For two weeks, the two of them were playing cross-country computer chess. Then the phone bill came in and Dad flipped.

"Joanne, you can't do this to me. You want to send me to the poorhouse?"

"Dad, you can afford it," she said.

"No, young lady. And neither can you. When you earn your own money, then you can spend it any way you want."

"All right, I'll restrict my communication to local access," she said. That was real hacker talk. Hackers didn't talk English. They talked Computer.

"You want some of this macaroni or not?" I said.

"Hold it." Her fingers were going a mile a minute. "What are you doing?"

"Chatmode."

There were a bunch of cheeps and squeaks coming from the computer. It sounded like she was talking to chipmunks. I went over and watched her. She typed, "WERE YOU IN SCHOOL TODAY? I DIDN'T SEE YOU."

Back came the answer: "I DIDN'T SEE YOU, EITHER. WHERE WERE YOU?"

"I CAME IN LATE," Joanne typed. "DID YOU DO THE HIDEOUS HOMEWORK?"

"Who's that?" I said.

"Ernie Paik. He's in my UG. User Group," she added before I could ask. "ERNIE, DID YOU SOLVE PROBLEM 10?"

39

"JOANNE, I THOUGHT YOU'D GET IT EASY." An algebraic formula appeared on the screen.

I leaned over Joanne's shoulder, put my paws on the keys, and typed, "ERNIE PAIK, HI, THIS IS GEORGE. I ALWAYS MEANT TO ASK IF YOU HAVE A SISTER IN HIGH SCHOOL."

"NO. AN AUNT."

"LILLIAN?"

"YES. SHE PLAYS THE FLUTE IN THE ORCHESTRA. DO YOU LIKE HER, GEORGE?"

"SHE'S A GOOD KID. SHE'S IN MY AMERICAN HISTORY CLASS."

"YOU GOT THE HOTS FOR HER?"

"MYOB. I'VE GOT A GIRLFRIEND."

"MAYBE YOU WANT TWO."

"Smartass kid, your friend Ernie," I said to Joanne.

"ERNIE," Joanne typed, "MY BROTHER THINKS YOU'RE A — "

"Joanne, you're asking for trouble."

" — SMART KID." Joanne gave me a smile. She signed off with Ernie. "GOTTA GO NOW, PAIK, MY BROTHER'S BOTHERING ME. SEE YOU TOMORROW."

"So that's what you do all the time in here," I said.

"No, I do a lot of stuff."

I sat down at the keyboard and Joanne sat next to me, eating the rest of the macaroni and showing me things she could do on the modem. There were communication boards she could hook into, a bulletin board where she could leave or pick up messages, and a storyboard where people either made up their own stories or added to someone else's. There were ways for people to share information or support each other when in trouble, talk, get things off their chests.

"See, George, it's not complicated. Anyone can get the hang of it. Even you."

"Bless you, my child."

"You know what I mean. You don't get your kicks out of computers."

I sat there, punching keys and trying to keep up with the rapid-fire instructions I was getting from Joanne. I caught about fifty percent of it. We were on the bulletin board when a message caught my attention.

"HELP. SMALL PRACTICAL PROBLEM. I WANT TO KILL MY DENTIST. ANY ADVICE FOR ME? SIGN-OFF, BLOOD AND GUTS."

"Who's going to answer that?" I asked Joanne.

"I don't know."

The answer appeared on the screen. "BLOOD AND GUTS, FOR GOOD HEALTH HABIT, AVOID DENTIST AT ALL COSTS."

"Now what happens?" I asked. "Will Blood and Guts answer?"

"Maybe she just left the message there and she'll come back later for an answer."

"She? You think Blood and Guts is a she?"

"Who cares? Maybe it's a he. Maybe it's an it. Maybe it's a Max Headroom. That's what I like about the modem, George. You can talk to anybody, and nobody cares *what* you are or *who* you are. I could be talking to the President, and he wouldn't know I was twelve years old and a girl and lived in Clifton Heights. All he'd know is what I said."

"And what would you say to the President?"

She punched me. "Don't give me that goofy, patronizing smile. I'd probably say something nice and soothing. He's got a hard job. He's got to relax some-

41

times. Maybe there are things he can't say to anyone else, because he's President and everybody thinks the Prez has to know all the answers. Probably he never gets a chance just to be silly, so I might tell him, 'Prez, you can be as silly as you want with me. I won't give it away.' "

Another message appeared.

"APPRECIATE CONCERN FOR MY HEALTH. DENTIST IS THE ONE I'D STILL LIKE TO CROWN. TEETH ARE AT THE ROOT OF THIS PROBLEM."

" 'Root of this problem,' " Joanne repeated. "Har-har-har."

"Shhh," I whispered.

"They can't hear us, George."

"B&G: INVITE DENTIST ON A LONG CRUISE IN A LEAKY BOAT. OR GET HIM DRUNK ON TOP OF THE WORLD TRADE CENTER. OR, ALL ELSE FAILING, TIE HIM TO THE BACK OF A TAXI AND SEND THE DRIVER TO CALIFORNIA."

"These people are really getting into it," I said to Joanne. "Do you think I could put something in?"

"Go ahead."

I typed, "PUSH HIM OFF ONE OF HIS BRIDGES." It was silly, but fun. I went on playing around with the modem, hooking into different conversations. Joanne left to make herself a milk shake.

Chapter 6

In the morning, before she left for work, my mother asked if Troy and I would pick up a bureau she'd left at the refinisher's. I buttered a roll, thinking about Julie. I'd dreamed about her last night. Something about a cat meowing and screeching . . . someone crying. It was a relief to wake up.

"Troy still has his truck, doesn't he?" my mother said.

I nodded. "He'll do it, Mom, if he doesn't have football practice." I waited. I knew what my mother was going to say next. *I can't understand why anyone with Troy's talent. . . .*

"George," Mom said, right on cue, "I can't understand why anyone who can play the piano like Troy would risk his fingers on a football field."

"Well, he likes football."

"But music is so much more satisfying."

"He likes that, too, Mom. He's got room for both in his life."

"I suppose so," my mother said doubtfully.

My parents' opinion of Troy as a musical genius was formed the day they came home and found him playing Beethoven at our piano. Nobody in our family knew how to play the piano like that. Given half a chance, my father would start in on how he'd always dreamed of playing the piano, and how he never had a chance to learn because he went to work in his father's barber shop when he was ten years old.

This speech always ended with, "If I'd had the opportunities you kids have, I would have practiced four hours a day every day of the year and considered it a rare privilege."

"Right, Dad." He and my mother had more or less forced me to take lessons when I was a kid, and they were pushing Joanne now. Neither of us had any talent for music. I was even more hopeless than Joanne. I never got past *Für Elise*. At least Joanne could play a few things.

So you can appreciate how my parents felt when they came home that day and saw Troy hunched over the keyboard, with those big mitts of his drawing the softest, most delicate sound out of the piano. He was totally involved in the music, his eyes closed, his hands like butterflies over the keys. Then his head snapped up, his hands rose, and he brought the sound up with big sweeping movements, a beautiful sound, more sound than we'd ever dreamed could come out of our piano.

My mother clapped.

"Bravo!" my father said.

"Where did you learn to play like that?" my mother said.

Troy stood up. "My mother's a piano teacher." There he was, my friend Troy the slob, shirt unbuttoned, belly showing above his pants. Ordinarily my parents would have noticed those things, clicked their tongues, wondered if this person was a good influence on their son. But Troy was forgiven all because of his rare talent.

"Beautiful," my father said, shaking Troy's hand. "You've got a wonderful talent."

After that, they always talked about him in a special way. And whenever he was at our house, they'd ask him to play the piano.

Troy came around the corner in his pickup, blasting the horn. "I hope you know I'm doing you an immense favor," he said as soon as I got in. He sucked up the last of a soda, then tossed the can on the floor.

"Understood. I'm humbly grateful." I booted some of the junk out of the way. The inside of his truck was like a giant wastebasket, ankle high in greasy hamburger papers, soda cans, and plastic cups.

We cruised over to Englewood. "George." Troy rapped me on the knee and pointed to some girls. "Pay attention. We're picking winners and losers here, hits and misses, stars and bombs, keepers and discards."

When it came to girls, there was always a certain cynical way guys talked. You didn't want to express emotion or show that you really liked a girl, or that you could be hurt or unhappy or vulnerable. Emotion was for girls. Guys were macho, impregnable. Iron forts. Any guy was superior to any girl. On higher

45

ground. Judging. Commenting. Ruling. Handing down the final verdict.

We'd be in the locker room after a workout in the gym and Troy would put an arm lock on me and drag me over to his locker and show me the latest naked lady. "What do you think?" He'd lick his lips and ask as if it were a serious question, "If you had the chance, would you?"

"Would I what?"

"If she invited you? Would you turn it down?"

I'd try to be cool about it. "Troy, you are a primo slimeball." And I'd tell him to get his head out from between his legs. But there'd be heat in my cheeks and my ears, and I knew that if he was a slimeball, so was I.

Now he pointed to a girl jogging by in sweats and a T-shirt. "Keeper or discard. I'd give her a nine, but she's a little light in the rear end."

"Duck walks turn me off, but my heart goes out to girls that are pigeon-toed."

"Is Julie pigeon-toed?"

"Tell her, and you're dead, man."

"You two — " He always said that, *you two*, and he never said it without a shake of his head that he reserved for anything that was almost beyond belief. Julie and I supposedly fit into that category. We weren't like other people, other couples. Not really normal.

Staying with one girl! How could I do it? Troy lusted over women. He liked to say, "I never saw a girl I didn't want to sleep with." Chris was a record for him. He'd been going with her for three months.

"Does Chris know you look this much?"

"She looks, too. Everybody looks."

46

"Julie doesn't."

Troy gave me a glance that said I was a poor, innocent jerk. "Everybody looks," he repeated. "And some of us do more than look."

"Meaning?"

"Meaning, Chris is great, but the world is full of girls. What am I supposed to do, retire at the age of seventeen?"

When we got to Englewood, we had trouble finding the refinishing shop. "It's called The Village Woodworker," I said. "Someone named Lydia Joy owns it." We finally located it on a small side street behind a row of expensive antique shops. Troy parked the truck and we got out. The door was locked. I rapped on the glass.

A black woman in a denim apron and jeans opened the door. She had high cheekbones, wore big glasses, and had her hair down around her shoulders. She was fairly beautiful.

"Good day," Troy said, turning on the charm.

"You have a bureau ready for Farina?" I asked.

"Farina?"

"That's my mother. She asked me to pick it up."

The woman looked at me, then at Troy. "And who's he?"

"He's my friend, here to help me carry it out. It's his truck." I indicated the pickup.

"Mmm," she said. "What's your phone number?"

I gave her the number of the shop. She left us standing outside while she phoned. She'd locked the door. When she came back, she let us in. "I've been robbed too many times," she said.

We followed Lydia Joy to the back of the shop,

where tables, chairs, and bureaus were stacked one on top of another. She stopped to tighten the clamps on a chair being reglued.

"Okay, three-drawer bureau. Here it is." She polished the top with a chamois. "It's a beautiful thing. Look at the grain." It was the first time there was some warmth in her voice.

"Oak," Troy said.

"No, it's not oak. It's chestnut," she said flatly.

I stooped down to look at the grain of the wood. Mom had bought the bureau at a house sale. It had been painted a dull brown and we'd all thought she'd thrown away her money.

"It's an unusual piece," Lydia Joy said. "There's very little chestnut around anymore." Then she gave us a lecture on how the chestnut trees once covered the eastern United States and supported a huge population of squirrels and other animals. And how today there wasn't a mature American chestnut left in the world. "Kids like you don't even know the difference."

"Well, you gave us something to think about," Troy said, with his usual sarcasm. She caught it, too.

I ran my hand over the top of the bureau. "It's like velvet."

"It should be. It's been sanded six times."

I looked around. I smelled raw wood, glue, and linseed oil. I liked seeing all this old, beat-up furniture piled up waiting to be worked on. "It must be great doing this work."

"Great? Only if you love it. There's no money in it, not the way I do it. See that piece over there?" She pointed to a large rolltop desk. "Some idiot painted that. It's over one hundred years old and it was nearly ruined. I've been working on it for months, and I still haven't gotten every speck of paint off. And when I do finish, you know what's going to happen? Someone will come in here, see it, want it, and then complain like hell about the price. They don't think anything about my labor. Okay, let's get this bureau out of here, boys."

Troy and I lifted the bureau and walked it back through the store. Outside, we loaded it in the back of the truck.

Then Lydia Joy climbed up and wrapped the chest in blankets and showed us how she wanted it tied down. "There's not a scratch on it now, and I don't want a scratch on it when you deliver it to your mom. Got that?"

"Got it," I said.

"We'll treat it like a newborn baby," Troy said.

I asked Lydia Joy if she did everything herself.

"You mean, all the work here? Yes. Why?"

"Oh. . . ." I smiled. "Just thought if you needed somebody to work for you — "

"You?"

"Yes."

"What are your qualifications?"

"I'm strong."

"You're not very big," she said.

That was kind of brutal. "Looks are deceptive," I said. "I'd really like to work here. I don't know, something about the wood and the smell . . . and making old things new." It sounded so lame, I stopped.

She looked at me. "I could use someone, but I need someone reliable. . . . Well, let me think about it."

"Which means no, meathead," Troy muttered.

But she took my name and number, scribbled it on a piece of paper, and stuck it in her pocket.

Later that day, I called Julie. Her mother answered. "George? I just walked into the house myself. I don't even have my shoes off. Let me see if Julie's here." When she came back, she said, "Julie wants to know if you got her letter."

"What letter?"

"I don't know, George. She said she sent you a letter."

"What'd she send me a letter for?"

"Wait a minute. . . . Julie!" She didn't bother covering the phone. "Do you want to talk to George? . . . Okay . . . George, all I know is she says you should have the letter by now."

"No, I don't."

"And she says she can't talk to you till you read the letter."

"I don't get it."

"I don't get it, either, George. Julie says, after you read it, then you'll understand. Okay, George?" She hung up.

A letter? From Julie? Why a letter? We didn't write each other letters. We were on the phone almost every day. The last time she had written to me was two years ago, the summer she went away for a month to visit her father's parents in Corpus Christi, Texas. The only thing I remembered from those letters was how boring and flat it was out there and how she couldn't wait to get back and see me.

What did she have to say that she couldn't say face-to-face? Something bad, I thought. And I remembered that dream about the cat and Julie.

50

I checked the front hall, the mail drop inside the door, and the window seat where my mother sometimes left the mail. There was an L. L. Bean catalogue and a flyer announcing a pancake breakfast. Was that today's mail or left over from another day?

I called my mother at work. "Mom, did you get the mail today?"

"You mean here? At the shop? Yes."

"Was there a letter for me?"

"No. Why?"

"How about the mail at home?"

"George. Darling. You're home, not me."

"There's no mail here."

"Then I guess it didn't come."

"Doesn't it come earlier than this?"

"I thought so. Are you sure there's no mail?"

"Mom, that's what I'm asking you!"

"Shh," she said, "not so loud. What's the trouble? What's supposed to come in the mail?"

"Nothing! Just a letter."

"Well, it'll come. Be patient. I have to go now, darling." She hung up.

I stood there for a moment. What is it, Julie? Why a letter? I remembered how angry she'd gotten at her mother the other night. Did it have something to do with that? That didn't make any sense. If she was mad at her mother, then she ought to write her mother a letter.

Suddenly I remembered a funny thing that Julie said to me a few weeks ago. "You always say 'understood.' I'm sick of hearing you say, '*Understood, understood*.'"

I didn't get it. "I always say what?"

"George, we're going shopping Saturday. Am I right?"

"Understood."

51

"There you go," Julie said. "Exhibit A."

I hadn't even heard myself say it. "I'll stop saying it if it bothers you," I said.

"Yes, it bothers me."

"Okay, fine. That's the end of that."

"Good." We didn't talk for a while. "I want to see a movie on Saturday," Julie said.

"Understood."

"But not that war movie. You know how I feel about war movies."

"Understood."

Julie grabbed my arm. "You just did it twice in a row. It's so obnoxious! And you know what, now I'm doing it, too. Every time someone says something to me, I catch myself saying 'Understood'! I can't stand it. Now we're even talking alike."

Understood. Understood. I went and looked for the mailman. *Understood,* she said. Only I wasn't understanding anything.

Chapter 7

"Joanne?" I yelled up the stairs to my sister's room. No answer. "Joanne, where are you?"

"Down here." Her voice floated up from the basement.

"Did the mail come?"

"I don't know."

"You didn't take it in?"

"No."

I went down to the basement room where my workout mats were stacked. Joanne and Ernie Paik were down there. Joanne was soldering some bits of wire together. Ernie watched intently. I'd never seen him look any other way. He didn't talk much, either. In fact, that "conversation" we had on the computer was the longest one I'd ever had with him. Come to think of it, I'd hardly ever seen him eat, either. Maybe that's why he looked dazed — undernourished — but maybe it was because he was on another plane, a higher level.

"Joanne," I said, "did you take the mail in?"

There was a hiss and Joanne blew gently on the joined part. "Told you no, George."

"Why not?"

"There's never anything for me."

"You didn't see the mail?"

"George! Negative."

I went upstairs and checked the mailbox again. Still empty. I didn't feel like eating. I called Troy. No answer. I went up to Joanne's room. Then I couldn't remember what I'd come up for. There was a bluish glow coming from her terminal. Joanne had left her computer on. After a while, I sat down and began playing with the keyboard. "UNDERSTOOD," I wrote. "I FEL BLAH. ALSOO BLAH BLEAGHH BLAHGH. AND BLAAAH BLAAUH BLAH BLAFLH BLAH."

I must have hit a key or a combination of keys. Things began to happen. Red lights blinked, the machine whirred. Words — not mine — appeared on the screen. "HOW DO YOU SPELL BLAA, ANYWAY? BLAH? OR BLAAGHH? OR BLAAAAAAAAAAH?"

"BLAH," I wrote. "AS IN THTS NICE END BLUGH." I was typing fast. "BLAAAAAAAAAAAH." I leaned on the Repeat key for that one. "MY SISTOR IS A COMPOTER NUT. WHT ABOUT YOURZ?"

"WHERE'D YOU LEARN TO SPELL?"

"I'M IN-TOO-ITIV. VOHCABULARRY BETTER THAN MY SPELL SKILLS."

"IN-TOO-ITIV, KNOW ANYTHING ABOUT ME?"

"YOU LIKE COMPUTERS," I tapped out.

"HO-HUM."

54

"MAYBE THAT WAS A LITTLE OBVIOUS."

"FOR AN INTUITIVE, YES."

To redeem myself I keyed in, "YOUR SISTER PLAYS THE PIANO AND SINGS." Wild guess. Very wild. He tapped back one word.

"WRONG."

"MY IN-TOO-ISHIN MUST HAVE SLIPPED. YOU PLAY PIANO AND SHE PLAYS A FLUTE."

"WRONG."

"YOU PLAY A FLUTE?"

"NO, A TIN WHISTLE."

"CLOSE. CLOSE. THEN YOUR SISTER IS A TUBA PLAYER."

"I WISH MY SISTER DID PLAY THE TUBA, ONLY I DON'T HAVE A SISTER. I HAVE 2 BROTHERS."

"YOU SHOULD HAVE A SISTER. EVERYBODY SHOULD HAVE A SISTER. DO YOU KNOW JOANNE?"

"WHO'S JOANNE?"

"THIS IS JOANNE'S COMPUTER. YOU'RE NOT ONE OF HER FRIENDS?"

"NOT ME."

"THIS IS A REE-DICK-U-LUS KON-VER-SAY-SHUN. WHAT'S YOUR NAME?"

"CALL ME ICEBOX. WHO ARE YOU?"

"CALL ME TOMBSTONE. WANT TO TALK DEATH AND DESOLATION?"

"YOU FEEL THAT BAD?"

Briefly I thought of Julie's letter. "I MAY FEEL WORSE SOON."

"DO YOU FEEL BAD A LOT?"

"NOT THAT OFTEN, ICEBOX. HOW ABOUT YOU?"

"SOMETIMES. I RECOMMEND LONG WALKS, LONG, HOT SHOWERS."

"NOT COLD SHOWERS?"

"THAT, TOO, AT THE RIGHT MOMENTS. ALSO, TALK-ING TO A FRIEND HELPS. IF YOU HAVE ONE. RIGHT NOW, I DON'T."

"I THOUGHT I HAD A FRIEND, ICEBOX. BUT SHE WON'T TALK TO ME TODAY. OR YESTERDAY, EITHER."

"WHAT'D YOU DO?"

"WISH I KNEW. SHE WROTE ME A LETTER. SAYS AFTER I READ HER LETTER I CAN TALK TO HER."

"UH-OH."

"EXACTLY, ICEBOX. UH-OH . . . IS YOUR NAME REALLY ICEBOX?"

"IS YOUR NAME REALLY TOMBSTONE?"

"NO, IT'S BEAUTY PARLOR."

"AND MINE IS TOP HAT. WHERE'D YOU GET THAT NAME? DO YOU WORK IN A BEAUTY PARLOR?"

"YOU MIGHT SAY I ALMOST OWN ONE."

"OWN YOUR OWN BUSINESS? ME, TOO, IN A MANNER OF SPEAKING."

Just then, Joanne came in. "Out, George. I want my room."

"GOTTA GO, TOP HAT. TALK TO YOU AGAIN. SIGNING OFF NOW."

"OK, THAT'S KOOL."

I got up from the computer. "It's all yours, Joanne."

"It always was," she said, giving me a push in the direction of the door.

Later, my mother called from work to say she had a letter for me at the shop. "I'll bring it home, George."

"When are you coming home?"

"You know we're open till nine tonight."

"I'm coming over."

Mom had taken the Bug, Dad had his car, and the only thing on wheels at home was my bike. When I got to Leonard's, Mom handed me a letter. I looked at my name written across the front in black ink. It was Julie's handwriting, all right. Why had she sent it here? And why no return address? I turned the envelope over. Nothing. Not a sign that it was from her.

I tucked it in my back pocket and left. I thought I was calm — I had the letter now, I'd read it, and that would be that — but I walked away and forgot my bike. It was only later, when I was already home, that I remembered where I'd left it.

As I walked, I took the letter out of my pocket, smoothed it, and studied the way Julie had written my name across the face of the envelope. For a person as well organized and neat as Julie, she had surprisingly big, loopy handwriting. I looked at everything on that envelope. I looked at the postmark and the stamp. A regular stamp with the American flag, but I noticed it was pasted on crookedly, as if Julie had slapped it on. Angrily? Hastily? Or had she been nervous, too?

She shouldn't have written me a letter, no matter what it was about. She should have told me whatever it was she had to say, straight to my face. I started to get mad, and instead of reading the letter I folded the envelope and put it in my breast pocket.

It was a long walk home. I could feel the letter riding in my pocket. It was almost like feeling Julie's hand against my skin, as if she were slowly rubbing the contents of the letter into me. Soon the message would move upward to my brain.

There were clouds overhead, moving with me. For a while I walked hard. I thought of hiking over to Liberty Mall. Julie would be at work. I'd wave the letter at her, then read it out loud. No. I'd read it silently, but I'd move my lips and give her plenty of significant looks in between.

The truth was, I was scared of the damn letter. Scared of a piece of paper with a handful of words. Did I know what it was going to say? If I did, it was somewhere in the far reaches of my brain, somewhere in the Siberia of my mind, a cold, cold place I knew was there, but that I couldn't reach.

Read the letter!

I turned around as if someone had spoken to me. Behind me, a woman in tight leather pants and a red tunic was talking to a small girl also in a red tunic. I drifted over to the other side of the street and leaned against a brick wall. An old man was standing opposite me near the entrance to Rite Aid. He was shabby, wearing house slippers. His lips were moving. Praying or talking to himself? I watched him for a while, wondering if he lived on the street or had someplace to go home.

Read the letter!

A cop got out of his covered tricycle and stepped into the middle of the road and stopped traffic. The woman in the leather pants crossed with the little girl. Then two old ladies in animal skin coats and flashing glasses crossed. The cop raised his right hand against the traffic; his left hand beckoned. The old man in house slippers shuffled across the street and settled himself in the doorway of the White Rose Laundromat. Praying again. For clean laundry? Maybe that was what I should do — pray.

Read the letter!

I crossed the street, went into the laundromat, and sat down by the window. I took the letter out of my pocket. I held it in my hand. The sun was bouncing off the window as I ripped open the envelope. Inside, there were three closely written pages.

Chapter 8

My dear George,

My dear George. What kind of opening was that? So formal, almost foreign. I never heard Julie talk like that. Did she think she was writing a business letter in school?

I've been wanting to say something to you for a long time.

Then why didn't you?

I've been trying to say this to you. It's hard for me to say it. No, I take that back. It's not really hard so much as —

Make up your mind, damn it, Julie; was it hard or was it easy?

I started the letter again.

My dear George,
I've been wanting to say something to you for a long time. I've been trying to say this to you. It's hard for me to say it. No, I take that back. It's not really hard so much as —

I couldn't get any farther. I couldn't keep reading. I kept talking back to Julie even before I finished a sentence. And I was sweating. The old man in house slippers had moved to the front of the dryers. He was still praying. Pray for me, old man. I stuffed the letter in my pocket and walked out. At the corner, I stopped, took the letter out, and read it quickly, straight through.

She wrote,

— not really hard so much as scary. It scares me to say what I need to say. So I've been cowardly and let things drag on.

George, every time I try to talk to you about this, something happens. I say something and you say something else, turn my words aside or turn them upside down and inside out. It's like a game, you catch my words and don't really listen to them and shoot them back to me, but they come back different, so, somehow, I'm not saying what I was saying.

But then again, maybe it's my own fault, maybe I'm just not saying plainly what I need to say.

That's why I'm writing this letter.

I wish I didn't have to do it this way. I know it's

cowardly, but I know if I look into your eyes, I'll never be able to say it.

Do you know what your eyes are like? You say my eyes are like the morning, like water, like the sea, like the sky. You say all those things. Well, your eyes are you. There you are, right there, all of you in your eyes. Your eyes — they seem to me to be sad and lonely and demanding. I don't know what your eyes are really saying — maybe this isn't true — but they always make me think you want something from me I'll never be able to give you.

Sometimes I've looked at myself, at my eyes, tried to see the things you see, but I never do. Eyes like water? Eyes like the sky? I look and I just see me, and somehow I wish that was what you saw, too. I'm not what you say I am. I'm not wonderful, George. I'm not an unearthly being. I'm not an object of love. I don't know exactly what I am, but I want to find out. And I don't want you to tell me what I am. Because that's only what you think I am — your Julie with eyes like the sky.

I can hear you now, protesting, saying in that impatient, energetic way of yours, "But Julie, I know who you are!"

No good, George, no good. It's no use your saying you know me — I have to find out about myself for myself.

Do you hear me, George? Do you know what I'm saying? It's like this. I made up my mind, finally. I'm going to say what I have to say. I tried the other night when you were at the house. It didn't work. I haven't said what I wanted to say a lot of times we've been together. I'm doing it now. I'm getting to it. I'm saying it one way and then I'm going to say it another way and then maybe I'll say it a third way or a fourth way, till you hear me.

The other night, remember, we talked about your father selling our house to the developers and I got a little mad at you? I let myself get mad at you because your father

61

has so much power over us. He can sell this house and we'd have to move and we can't do anything about it. I know that's unfair, it has nothing to do with you. Your father was just an excuse to get mad, because I didn't have the guts to say what I really wanted to say. I was afraid for you. Afraid for me. Afraid for us.

George, you've been my best friend for a long time. I don't want to lose that. That's what I'm afraid of. But I don't want to end up hating you, either.

And I'm beginning to feel that way. Hating you. Hedged in. Imprisoned. We go out every weekend. We talk on the phone every day. I don't do anything, make any decisions, without talking to you first. We've got all these routines. I used to love them. They were like little fences around the two of us, closing us off from the rest of the world. It was cozy and comforting. Now they're like bars. And I hate them. I want those bars down.

I'm calling off this weekend's plans. And next weekend and the weekend after. I'm calling off our daily phone calls. I'm canceling our consultations and our walks and everything else that went along with all that.

This doesn't mean I don't want to see you at all. Or that I want to be by myself. I might want to see other people. I do want to see other people, including other boys.

There, I said it. That was the hard part, the hardest thing, the part I've been feeling most cowardly about saying to you.

I know you're feeling hurt reading this, and I don't want to hurt you. Can you believe that? I don't want to hurt you. I tried to tell you, to prepare you the other night when we were doing the dishes. You didn't listen. Or you didn't hear. Or you didn't want to hear. Maybe all three.

I love you, George, I've loved you since I was twelve years old. But we're not twelve anymore, or thirteen or

62

fourteen. I'm seventeen and I want to meet other people and I want to meet myself. Alone. Without you. Just Julie. I want to say, "Hi, Julie! Hello there, Julie, what kind of person are you without George?"

Can you understand this, George? I hope so!

Love, Julie.

I started walking again. My stomach tightened as if I were about to throw up. Phrases kept running through my mind. *I know you're feeling hurt. . . . I'm calling off this weekend . . . and the weekend after. . . . but we're not twelve anymore . . .*

I didn't get it. What was this all about? She wanted to meet herself? What kind of crap was that? She was right about one thing and one thing only. I *could* tell her what kind of person she was, if that was what she wanted to know. She was loving, warm, intelligent, directed. She was sensitive — or so I used to think. How sensitive could she really be if she sent me a letter like this, a bolt from the blue, for no reason. She said she'd tried to tip me off. Had she, really? I wasn't that thick. I would have caught on. She was, just as she'd said, scared to do it. And why? Because she knew she was wrong.

Why should we stop seeing each other just because she had some screwy ideas right now? If she didn't want to go out this weekend, that was cool with me. Or next weekend or whatever. I wasn't her master, we didn't sign a contract, we didn't have that kind of relationship. All she had to do was say, "George, let's loosen up a little. Lighten up." She didn't have to like me every minute. I didn't have to like her every minute. I'd gotten mad at her plenty of times. Only I always knew that it was temporary, that it was going to blow over, and that behind being mad was the way I really felt about her.

Maybe she was kidding herself, and she really was stewing because of the house. My father never would sell the building, but she didn't know that. She was scared for her family. I could understand that. But was our not seeing each other a cure? It was like cutting off your head because you had a headache.

The more I thought about it, the more I thought she couldn't possibly have meant all the things she'd written. By now she'd had time to think things over. She'd probably cooled off. Maybe she was already feeling remorseful and was just waiting for me to call her.

In an outside phone booth, I dialed Buzzy's. "Julie isn't here today."

I hung up and dialed the Walshes. Nobody answered. I dug for more change, found the number of Julie's school, dropped the coin in the slot, and dialed. The phone rang for a long time. I knew it was stupid, a lost cause, but I let it ring. I finally got a janitor, who told me the office was closed. "There's still some people here, activities, but the office is closed till tomorrow."

"Would you know if Julie Walsh is there?"

"No."

"She isn't?"

"I don't know her."

"Tall girl, dark-haired."

"That's half the girls in the school."

I walked over to my school. Parts of the letter kept going through my head. *I want to meet other people.* I walked fast. I went over to the field and watched Troy at football practice. I hung on the fence, felt my bones stretch in their sockets, remembered how when I was

64

little I used to hang on the clothes pole in the closet to make myself taller.

It was a rough, hard practice. The Varsity against the Redshirts, the hopefuls, every one of them trying to impress the hell out of the coaches. Troy's shoulder pad was poking out of his shirt. He was poised on the line like a charging bull.

I want to meet other people.

The whistle blew. The coach was on a platform, calling the plays. Troy was hit by a defender. For a moment they hung on each other, then Troy broke away and charged toward the ball carrier.

"Hit him!" I yelled. "Grab him! Cream him! Waste him!" I slapped the fence. *I want to meet other people.* If only I was there, on the other side of the fence, cutting off the runner, hitting him low. "Hit him, Troy. Hit that boy. No mercy!" Troy caught the runner by the ankle and brought him down. "Yes!" I cried. "Yes!"

Chapter 9

My first reaction to Julie's letter had been anger, fear and anger. But by the next morning, I'd cooled down. I had the anger under control and channeled. I knew Julie. She got passionate about ideas, got carried away, talked like she was going to change her life. This wasn't the first time. What about her volunteer work in an old people's home? Two days working there, and she was going to spend the rest of her life helping old people. She was sincere, she meant it when she said it, but a couple of months later she was equally passionate and equally sincere about becoming a veterinarian. And now she was being sincere and passionate about separating her life from mine.

What you're going to do, I told myself, is wait.

You're going to wait a few days and not do anything. Wait a week if you have to. You're not going to call Julie. You're not going to try to talk to her. You're going to give her time. You're not going to make demands. That's step one. It's going to blow over, you just have to be patient.

It's easy enough to give yourself advice, but following it is the hard part. One day without Julie, two days without Julie. . . . Three days without Julie, and I was talking to myself. Four days and I didn't want to wait anymore. Wasn't four days long enough? Why hadn't Julie called me by this time to say the letter was a mistake, a big, fat, ridiculous blunder?

I'd been going straight home from school so I could be there when she called. *George? Did you read that stupid letter I wrote you? George! Throw it away!* I hung around the house, afraid to be away from the phone. Waiting. Thinking about nothing but Julie. "You keep that up and you'll grind a track in the rug," my mother said one evening, after I'd paced the hall, heel to toe, for the hundredth time.

"Sorry. I'll stop." But a moment later, I was pacing again.

"What's the trouble?" my mother said.

I watched her draw the drapes, a ritual with her when she got home from work. First the drapes, then the lights went on everywhere in the house. "Nothing, Mom. It's okay." I stared at the phone on the table.

She turned on a few more lights and sat down on the couch. "George." She made a place for me next to her. "You want to tell me?"

"No, Mom, it's not something I want to talk about."

"You sure? You look so toubled, George."

I was too old to cry on my mother's shoulder. What could I say? Julie told me to get lost? Or should I say, *Mom, you may think your son is terrific, but Julie has other ideas.*

"George, the last time you looked so tragic was when Fuzzy died."

"Fuzzy!" I laughed abruptly. Fuzzy was the Abyssinian guinea pig I'd had when I was nine years old. So I looked now the way I had when my guinea pig kicked the bucket. The same expression for Julie as for Fuzzy. No wonder Julie was looking around for someone else. "Thanks for putting things back in perspective," I said. How bad could my troubles be? Did they stack up to losing Fuzzy? Were they worse than something that happened to me when I was nine years old? I was seventeen now, but so what? I had the big tragedy of my life when I was nine years old!

"I was just trying to cheer you up."

"And you succeeded, Mom." I gave her what I hoped was a cheerful expression but which probably came out like a dying man's grimace.

"You loved that little guinea pig," my mother said. "He had to sleep by your bed. You talked to him all the time. Took great care of him. It was amazing, we never had to remind you to feed him or give him water or anything."

"I was a nice little kid. Too bad I had to grow up."

"Oh, you're not so bad now. You're pretty terrific, I'd say."

"Only a mother would say that."

"I'm sure there's at least one other person who feels the same way."

"Who?" My head sank into my hands.

"You had a fight with Julie, didn't you?"

I nodded.

"You'll make up with her. I'm sure you've had fights and disagreements before."

"Right, Mom." I said it, but what I thought was, Yes, we've had spats, little things, but nothing like this. Nothing, ever, like this.

That was a tough week. I found it hard to concentrate on anything. I spent a lot of time thinking about Julie, about the good times we'd had together. The last couple of years we didn't climb around the cliffs the way we used to. Sometimes, depending on how we felt (horny) or the weather (rainy or cold), we'd go up to the Walshes' apartment, eat and do homework, and whatever. . . . I won't say we didn't fool around. Of course we did. But it wasn't the awful stuff some people made it out to be.

Mrs. Adams, the Walshes' downstairs neighbor, had her antennae out for us. Even before we entered the house, we'd see the curtains at her window moving. "Hello, Mrs. Adams!" Julie would wave. In the hall, Mrs. Adams' door was to our left. No sooner were we past than the downstairs door would fly open and Mrs. Adams would pop out in her pink rabbit slippers. "Uh-huh!" she would say loudly.

"Hello, Mrs. Adams," Julie would say sweetly, and she'd whisper to me, "One of these days, I'm going to tell Pink Rabbit to mind her own business!"

One day, Julie's mother got us both together and said, "I hear you two are going up to the house every day."

"Who told you that?" Julie said.

"Mrs. Adams. She says you're up there for hours and that you make a great deal of, uh, unusual noise."

Julie and I looked at each other. "Mom," Julie said, "did you tell her to butt out?"

"What are you kids doing, anyway? She says — "

"Mom! I live here. I don't have to explain what I'm doing in my own house."

"Not to Mrs. Adams, that's true, but I'm interested."

"What'd she tell you? What kind of smut did she say? You believe her? That silly woman. Why shouldn't we come up here? I live here and George is my friend."

"Yes, but what are you doing?" her mother repeated.

"Eating," I said. I'd been waiting to put in my two cents.

"George," Julie said. "That is not exactly true."

"Julie, you know your mother is a fantastic cook." I loved raiding their refrigerator. There was no such pleasure raiding the Farina refrigerator, unless you liked attacking frozen dinners with an ice pick. "Really, Mrs. Walsh, lots of times, all we do is stuff our faces."

"Will you shut up, George." Julie's cheeks were red. As she told me later, she didn't see any reason for us to be defensive. She was mad that her mother didn't trust her enough not to ask questions. "Mom, whatever we're doing, as long as we're not burning down the house, you don't have to worry. We're old enough to take care of ourselves."

"Well, I'm sure you are, but — "

"No buts! I know what I'm doing, Ma," Julie said. She was aroused and bouncing around, pointing a finger at her mother. "You have to impress your children. . . . I mean, depress . . . repress. . . ." She was so agitated she couldn't find the right word. "Bust . . . lust . . . lust . . . trust," she finally exclaimed. "Trust! Trust your children."

70

Later, Julie and I laughed about it. How agitated she got, how she kept saying the wrong word. "You kept saying 'lust,' " I said. "Lust. Your mother knew what was on your mind."

Actually, her mother was pretty relaxed about the whole thing. I think she did trust us. At least she let the subject drop, and she didn't come up with any kind of changes in the rules. But one thing didn't change. Mrs. Adams went right on watching us. Even that was something that bound Julie and me together. We were the ones who knew about the Pink Rabbit. It was one of our private jokes. We had a lot of them, a whole history together, a whole history behind us. We'd been friends and in love longer than some people had been married. I'd believed that nothing could ever break Julie and me apart.

Had I been so wrong? So mistaken? I waited for her to call me, to say in her light, beautiful voice, "George, what are you doing?" I was waiting for that moment, so I could be happy again.

Then, one day I stopped waiting. The letter she had written was like a web she had spun, and I had let myself be caught in it. The story she'd made up for not wanting to see me wasn't my story. It was her story. She had given it an air of fate, as if it was preordained, as if these things were happening now because we had committed a basic error. We'd found each other too early, too young, too soon.

That day I called Julie three times. Her sister answered every time. "Not home, George," she said. I called an hour later. "Julie's taking a nap." And again, after supper. "No, George."

Now that I'd broken my wait-and-cool-it rule, I broke it with a vengeance. I called in the morning before school. I called after school. I called before supper and after supper and again when the eleven o'clock news came on.

Beth took to sighing every time she heard my voice. "Sorry, George."

"Listen, Beth, don't be so sorry; just get Julie to the phone."

"Wait a minute," she said. Only it sounded like "wade-a-minni. . . ." She was sick of answering the phone. All I did was call and all she did was make excuses. "Julie's sleeping. . . . She's showering. . . . She's not available."

"Beth, tell your sister she's not going to get rid of me this easily. I'll keep calling till I get her." I'd be like a fly on the phone. *Bzzz-bzzz-bzzz.* I'd make even more of a pest of myself than I had already. I'd call every twenty minutes. I'd call at two minutes past midnight and four minutes to three and again at six in the morning. *I'm sorry, Mr. Walsh, Mrs. Walsh, and Beth, I surely didn't mean to wake you, I know you have to work in the morning, I know this isn't an answering service, but do you know this is a matter of life and death? Yes! My life. My death. Julie is killing me.*

And what would they say then? *Oh, poor George. . . . Let me check. . . . No, sorry, George, Julie just this minute stepped out. . . .*

At three in the morning?

It wasn't only Beth who delivered the excuses. Sometimes her mother answered. Once, her father. Another time, her Aunt Patty was visiting and *she* got on the phone. "Do you want to leave a message? Julie's out shopping now."

Sure she was. Julie was never in, never available.

72

Not to me. Was I being paranoid to think it was a family conspiracy? *Sorry, George, Julie just went to the store. . . . She's showering . . . She's working tonight . . . washing her hair . . . indisposed. . . .*

Indisposed? What did that mean? She was sick? Or she was in the bathroom? According to her family, she lived half her life in the bathroom. "Did she get my message? Does she know I called?"

"I think so." Beth sounded sympathetic, even apologetic, but she didn't get Julie to the phone.

"Tell her I'll call tomorrow."

"Will do."

Off the phone, I felt humiliated. What was I doing to myself? Begging, bleeding, pleading. Where was my pride, my indignation, my self-respect, my maleness, my he-ness, my authority? I deepened my voice. I practiced.

"Beth, tell Julie to call me. I'm going to wait half an hour. That's it. This is her last chance!" No, too strong. Try again. "Tell Julie I'll call back in half an hour. . . . Tell Julie if she doesn't come to the phone this time. . . ."

No, no, no. You're not going to make a fool of yourself. Just stop calling her. Put an end to this. Never call again. *"Auf Wiedersehen,* Julie. Farewell, my love. Farewell, forever." I wiped the tear that trickled from the center of my eye. Pleading, threatening, being ironic, then bleeding for myself. All strategies of defeat.

I walked away from the phone. I felt aggressive, frustrated, full of uncentered energy. I stopped at Joanne's room. "Joanne," I said, "come away from that damn computer! Look at the way you're sitting there. You're

73

getting to look more like a turtle every day. You can't build muscle sitting at a computer." I took her arm. "Come on, let's work out a little."

"I don't want to. I'm busy."

"Joanne, I'm doing this for you, not for me." I dragged her away. I was unfair, a little crazy, too. Poor Joanne. I got a cross-body hold on her and I pulled her to the stairs, babbling about self-defense and being in control. This was all for her own good.

My sister didn't take it graciously. She was kicking at me, grunting, trying to break loose.

"You're a scrapper, that's good. Get down, Joanne, center yourself, keep your arms next to your body. Head back. Don't be a turtle."

She tried to kick my feet out from under me. She would have killed me if she could.

"Go for my middle. Toss me over your shoulder." She lunged at me. "That's good," I said. "Try to get through me." And then somehow, *bang*, she was under me and tossed me against the wall. The chimes bonged. My head rapped against the hall table. Over it went and everything that was on it, and Joanne was on top of me, sitting on me, her cheeks pink, her braid coming undone.

"Pinned you," she crowed. "Pinned you!"

That's when my parents walked in. They looked at the two of us on the floor, at the overturned table, the phone, the scattered mail. "What is going on here?" my father said. "What are you two doing? Why are you wrestling with your sister?"

"I pinned him," Joanne said. "I pinned big-mouth George!"

I pushed her off me and got up. "Okay, Mom and Dad. Nothing to get excited about. You guys walk

74

through as if you don't see anything."

"I don't see anything." My mother picked her way to the closet, hung up her coat, and went upstairs.

"Look at the mess here," my father said.

"I'm cleaning up." I put the table upright and the phone back and straightened the pictures on the wall.

My father's jaw stuck out half a mile. "How many times have I told you not to horse around with your sister? You're seventeen and you don't know yet that you shouldn't fight with girls?"

"That's stupid," I said. "I'm not fighting with her. I'm teaching her — "

"Stupid? You said stupid?"

"That's not what he means, Daddy." Joanne tried to cover for me. "George means — "

My father wasn't listening. He must have had a tough day. It wasn't like him. He turned on Joanne, whom he never yelled at. Never. "What did I buy you a computer for? So you could horse around and wrestle with your brother like someone off the streets? And you, my son! Don't you think about anybody but yourself? A man should be able to come home, relax, have a little peace and quiet."

"I said I was sorry!" All of a sudden, I got really upset. I started to say something else, but then I just shut up and walked away.

"Where are you going? I'm still talking to you."

I stopped, and he gave it to me some more, really loaded me up. He got it off his chest and on my head. "You got anything to say?" he asked finally.

I shook my head. By that point I was feeling so sorry for myself I could barely talk. "I'm going for a walk," I said and I went out.

I walked, and without realizing what I was doing, I

found myself at Julie's house. It was dark. The lights were on in the Walshes' windows. I leaned against the stone wall overlooking the cliff, and watched Julie's window. Would she know I was out here? Could she sense it? I'd stood in that same spot other times, beaming messages at her, and after a while, she had always looked out her window and seen me. Then, later, she would tell me she didn't know I was there, she had no idea, just a feeling that she wanted to look out the window.

Julie. Julie. Come to the window. Julie. Julie . . . don't you know how much I miss you. . . . Can't you sense that I'm here . . . waiting for you . . . Julie. . . .

I searched the window for her face. She'd see me, open the window and. . . . What would she say? Maybe just my name. *George.* That would be enough for me. And I'd say her name. *Julie.*

I stood there for an hour waiting for her, waiting for that moment. It never came.

I went around to the side of the house, made a leap for the fire escape, and went up the ladder till I was standing outside Julie's window.

To my right, across the river, there were the lights and lit-up sky of New York City. And through the window there was Julie, sitting cross-legged on the bed with books and a notebook in front of her. I crouched on the landing. My shirt was hiked up and I felt the wind on my back. I didn't move. I just looked at her, watched her, felt how much I loved her, how much I'd missed seeing her, talking to her, hearing her voice. Sometimes she looked up, turned in my direction, seemed to look straight at me. Then she'd look down at her books again.

I don't know how much time passed. Once, twice,

several times I felt myself leaning forward and my knuckles went up to the glass, and then I pulled back. It was as if the glass were more than glass.

Julie never came to the window. She didn't see me. She didn't sense my presence. She was inside and I was outside, and for the first time since I'd gotten her letter, I felt that we were truly separated and there was nothing I could do to bridge the gap between us.

Chapter 10

I was coming out of the post office when I ran into Julie. We almost walked into each other. I registered the surprise on her face and shifted the package I'd picked up to my other arm. "Julie!" She had a scarf around her neck and I gave it a little tug. "Great to see you!" I gave her a big greeting, as if I'd been smiling ever since I'd gotten her letter. And she smiled back.

I thought that in just these couple of weeks, she'd gotten thinner and better-looking. I couldn't stop looking at her and smiling and talking too much. "This is unexpected, right? What do we do now? This isn't part of the game plan." I was friendly and a little ironic, talking freely, being more open and cheerful than I really felt. "Do we talk to each other? Or do we keep going and act like we didn't see each other? I could close my eyes, proceed on, and make believe I never saw you."

Julie put down the bag she was carrying. "George, why shouldn't we talk? No, I'm glad we ran into each other. I want to know how you are. What are you doing these days?"

I held the package over my head. "Delivery boy. As you can see."

"You're working?"

"Well, let's not go overboard. No, this is for Mom. How about you?"

"Oh, I'm the same." She shifted from one foot to the other.

I felt her getting ready to leave. "What about a gelato?" I said quickly. There was a shop across the street.

She hesitated for a moment. "I have to be at work in an hour."

"You'll get there." I took her arm, although I didn't know if that was allowed or not. But how could I be so close to her and not even touch her? The gelato store was empty. We sat at a little round table in the window and ate raspberry gelatos.

"So how's life?" I said, smiling a little.

"Oh. Fine." She looked at me, then looked away. She wasn't exactly furtive, but she wasn't drinking up my face, either. "I'm keeping busy."

"Enjoying yourself?"

"Sometimes."

"Like your new life?"

"My new — ? Oh, you mean — " She half-smiled. "Not always — are you glad to hear that? But I'm not sorry, if that's what you want to know."

"I am." I stared at her. I had a full spoon raised to

my lips and there it stayed. "I'm sorry," I said. I threw off the smiling, cheerful idiot disguise. "I'm very sorry."

Julie had her hand on her cheek, her head cocked, held back as if she didn't want to look at me directly. "Why be so sorry? This gives you a chance, too, a chance to do things differently."

I moved my chair closer to hers and slipped my arm around her. I didn't want to hear about the letter again. "I missed you," I said, and I kissed her. I had some movie image of myself in mind. You know, the old you-can-talk-and-talk-but-actions-speak-louder-than-words bit. I kissed her. I didn't think she held back. I thought her kiss was as strong as mine. I put my hand over hers, and when we stopped kissing there was that soft swimmy look on her face. So I kissed her again, or tried to, but this time she pulled away.

"Sorry," I said.

"You're not," she said. "You're not sorry a bit."

"You're right."

She pushed her chair back. "You still don't understand, do you, George?"

"No, I don't. I don't know what that letter was all about. I don't know what kind of craziness you're up to. All I know is I miss you and I think you miss me. The way you just kissed me — "

"You don't want to understand," she said. "You want what you want, and you're not even thinking about what I tried to tell you or what I want."

I was smiling at her, holding on to that smile, holding on to the idea that the kiss had told me everything I needed to know. "Julie — come back."

"George, I can't. Don't ask me."

"Julie, please — "

"George, I have to go. I don't want to be late for work."

We walked outside together. "See you around, then," I said.

"Are we friends?" Julie said. "I want to stay friends, George."

"I don't know," I said. "I don't know if I want to be *friends* with you."

"We're friends," she said.

"Sure," I said, and I walked away.

When Troy first started going with Chris, he used to ask me questions about Julie. How had we managed to stay together so long? Was it sex? What about sex? Didn't it get dull with the same person? What did we talk about? From which I gathered that he liked Chris a lot and was wondering how long they would last.

He claimed he couldn't understand me and Julie, the mystery of the two of us together for so many years. How could I go with one girl so long without being bored out of my skull? "You're together all the time . . . in her house. . . . Well, that's it, then. You're one horny cat." He gave me an evil look, as if now he knew everything. It was sex. Had to be. What else could make a guy stay with a girl not just month after month, but year after year? Sex — that's what it was.

"You and Julie," he said once.

"Yeah, me and Julie, what?"

"Nothing, forget it." But then he said suddenly, with that open-faced look, "I envy you."

Once I thought I was worth envying.

And another time he asked me, "What do you really think about Julie?"

"I like Julie." It was such a limp thing to say. *Like* Julie? I liked bluefish. I liked my suede jacket. I liked to drive my father's car. Liked? *I like Julie?* It wasn't a pimple on the real feeling I had for her.

Now, though, when I told Troy I wasn't seeing Julie anymore, he didn't say anything comforting. "You've joined the human race." That was all. Didn't ask why, what, or anything.

I was home, restless, couldn't stand my own thoughts, and went into Joanne's room to play with the computer. I got Top Hat back on the chatmode. We "talked." Nothing much as far as I was concerned. Stuff that didn't matter. Killing time stuff.

"BEAUTY PARLOR, TELL ME TWO THINGS YOU HATE."

"WHY?"

"WANT TO FIND OUT ABOUT YOU. OKAY?"

"I HATE . . . NOT KNOWING WHAT'S GOING TO HAPPEN TOMORROW. LETTERS THAT DON'T ARRIVE. WRONG NUMBERS. GUYS WHO NEVER HAVE PROBLEMS. I COULD GO ON. HOW ABOUT YOU, TOP HAT?"

"EMPTY ROOMS. DOGS. GREEN-PLAID PANTS."

"I CAN'T STAND THE SIGHT OF BLOOD."

"YOUR OWN OR OTHER PEOPLE'S BLOOD?"

"ANYONE'S. I'D NEVER MAKE A GOOD DOCTOR."

"BEAUTY PARLOR, HOW CAN YOU BE FEMALE AND HATE YOUR OWN BLOOD?"

Female? I stared at the screen. *Female?* My own blood? I didn't get it, and then I did.

Top Hat thought I was a girl.

Where did he get that idea? From my handle? Beauty Parlor? Because, presumably, only girls didn't like the sight of blood? What about nurses? Or was it something about the way I said things? I thought about that for a moment and rejected it. I didn't have any problems about being a boy. No identity crises.

Then something else occurred to me. Why was I so sure Top Hat was a he? Was this a double case of wrong assumptions? Was he, Top Hat, a he, or what? Maybe what we had here was a "he" (Top Hat) who was a she, and a "she" (me) who was a he.

This was a nice mix-up.

"TOP HAT, FOR YOUR INFO, I'M NOT A. . . ." And then I stopped, went back, deleted it. Because there was something embarrassing about this whole situation, yes, but something intriguing, too. I started over again, playing around, playing for time, playing it by ear. "HOW ABOUT YOU? HOW DO YOU FEEL ABOUT BLOOD?"

"DOESN'T BOTHER ME."

"DON'T KNOW WHY, BUT I'VE ALWAYS BEEN THAT WAY ABOUT BLOOD. HAD A NOSEBLEED ONCE AND PANICKED. JULIE MADE ME LIE DOWN ON THE FLOOR AND PACKED TOILET PAPER INTO MY NOSE."

"WHO'S JULIE? YOUR SISTER?"

"BEST FRIEND. GIRLFRIEND." Not exactly a lie. No, it wasn't a lie at all. But it was less than the truth. "AT LEAST SHE USED TO BE MY BEST FRIEND."

"WHAT HAPPENED?"

"YOUR GUESS IS AS GOOD AS MINE."

"YOU HAD A FIGHT?"

"NO, I COULD UNDERSTAND THAT. SHE JUST DECIDED WE'D BEEN FRIENDS LONG ENOUGH."

"JUST LIKE THAT? SOUNDS PRETTY COLD-BLOODED TO ME. WERE YOU FRIENDS A LONG TIME?"

"SIX YEARS. CAN WE CHANGE THE SUBJECT? I'M STILL

HURTING OVER THIS." Then Joanne appeared, and I signed off. "HAVE TO GO NOW. MY SISTER, THE COMPUTER OWNER, IS HERE."

"TALK TO YOU TOMORROW, BEAUTY PARLOR?"

"COULD BE."

Later, thinking about Top Hat, I couldn't pinpoint anything in the conversation that would prove "he" was a boy . . . or a girl. So the mystery remained. Then I thought how I'd let him/her or her/him go on believing that *I* was a girl. I felt a little funny about it. But I hadn't done it deliberately. I hadn't out-and-out lied. I'd just neglected a few facts. If we ever talked again, I'd set it straight. Or not. Depending on how I felt.

Anyway, the mix-up and the mystery added an element of spice and kookiness to the situation that intrigued me. Made me look forward to talking to Top Hat again. I suppose what I liked was the game element. The idea of: Who was Top Hat? And could I do it again? Could I keep it going? Get away with having Top Hat believe I was a girl?

Well, it wasn't world-shaking, but it was something to think about, and its big virtue was that it was something-not-Julie to think about.

Chapter 11

"WHERE DO YOU LIVE?" Top Hat asked.

"OVER THE G. W. BRIDGE."

"NEW JERSEY?"

"HOW'D YOU GUESS?" I two-fingered out, "AND YOU?"

"NEW YORK CITY."

"CITY MOUSE AND COUNTRY MOUSE."

"IS JERSEY LIKE THE COUNTRY?"

"WELL . . . NOT EXACTLY," I said. "BUT IT'S SURE NOT NEW YORK."

"OR CHAMPION, EITHER."

"WHERE'S THAT?"

"ILLINOIS. WHERE I COME FROM. I'M REALLY A COUNTRY HICK."

Male hick? Female hickess?

"WHAT'S NEW JERSEY LIKE?" Top Hat said. "I'VE NEVER BEEN THERE, JUST HEARD PLENTY OF NEW JOISEY JOKES."

"JOISEY IS JUST FINE. IT'S MY HOME AND I LIKE IT."

* * *

Talking to Top Hat was a game, a game of wits, a guessing game. How much could I tell, being absolutely truthful — well, pretty truthful — and still not give away the game? How much could I say and not clue him/her in that she/he was talking to George Farina?

"BEAUTY PARLOR, WHAT DO YOU LOOK LIKE?"
Would a guy ask me that?
"I DON'T HAVE A BEARD. OR A MUSTACHE. OR HAIR ON MY CHEST."
"I SHOULD HOPE NOT. WHAT ELSE?"
"DARK-HAIRED."
"TALL?"
"NO."
"AVERAGE?"
"SHORT."
"THIN?" Top Hat asked.
"NOT PARTICULARLY."
"PRETTY?"
"NOT AT ALL." Was "he" disappointed?
"ARE YOU BEING MODEST?"
"TRUTHFUL. NO ONE EVER CALLED ME PRETTY."
George, you're getting good at this.
"BEAUTY PARLOR, BEING PRETTY IS NOT THE MOST IMPORTANT THING IN THE WORLD. TAKE IT FROM ME."
"ARE YOU PRETTY?" Now you're getting to it, George.
"SOME PEOPLE SAY I'M WEIRD, SOME PEOPLE SAY I'M WIRED."
Weird female? Wired male? Or vice-versa?
"ARE YOU SHORT?" I asked.
"TALL."
"HOW TALL?"
"FIVE ELEVEN-AND-A-HALF."

86

Five eleven-and-a-half? That settled it. Male.

"ARE YOU A BASKETBALL PLAYER?" I asked.

"NOW AND THEN. HOW ABOUT YOU?"

"THAT'S NOT MY SPORT."

"I DON'T PLAY ANY GAMES NOW. I JUST DANCE."

Dance? That settled it. Female. But maybe not. Guys danced, too.

"DO YOU HAVE A BOYFRIEND?" Top Hat asked.

"FRIEND WHO IS A BOY, YES." Clever, George. "A FOOTBALL PLAYER AND A PIANO PLAYER."

"YOU'VE GOT TWO BOYFRIENDS?"

"NO, JUST ONE."

"A FOOTBALL PLAYER WHO PLAYS THE PIANO? OR IS IT A PIANO PLAYER WHO PLAYS FOOTBALL?"

"EITHER WAY."

"IS HE SEXY?"

What did I say to that? "NOT TO ME."

"WHAT KIND OF BOYFRIEND IS HE, THEN?"

"ORDINARY. WE'RE GOOD FRIENDS, THAT'S ALL."

A good thing Joanne was a sound sleeper because I was in her room every night that week, hacking it with Top Hat. My parents' light was out. The house was dark, quiet; the only thing to be heard was the low hum of the computer, the quiet clicking of the keys.

"BEAUTY PARLOR, YOU THERE?" Top Hat came on. No hi's, no hello's, no how are you's. This was shooting straight from the hip. "BEAUTY PARLOR! HOW DO YOU FEEL ABOUT YOUR PARENTS?"

"ON A SCALE OF 1 TO 10? MY DAD'S ABOUT A 7. MY MOM'S AN 8½. WHY?"

"MY FATHER'S A 2 TODAY! HE WAS SUPPOSED TO BE HOME AND HE'S NOT HERE. I SHOULD HATE MY FATHER. I WISH I DID. I CAN'T. PITIFUL 2!"

87

"HOW ABOUT YOUR MOTHER?"

"DON'T LIVE WITH MY MOTHER. SHE'S REMARRIED. I HATE MY STEPFATHER. HE'S A MINUS SIXTY-SIX. DON'T WANT TO TALK. DEPRESSED. SIGNING OFF NOW."

I didn't tell anyone about Top Hat. We were computer pals, we had an electronic relationship, something separate and apart from my everyday life. Someday I'd tell Julie about it. *I made a friend, Julie, a very good friend. After all, it wasn't so bad being without you. I made this friend, this computer nut, this hacker, this ghost in the machine, this guy-gal, this he-she, this dancer, this weird, wired someone I was getting to really like without even knowing if it was a he-someone or a she-someone. . . .*

And does it matter?

One night, on chatmode with Top Hat, I started talking about Julie. I don't know why. Maybe I just wanted to walk the edge. Or maybe I wasn't thinking anything, just needed to talk about her.

"I HAVE THIS FRIEND."

"ANOTHER GUY?"

George, you almost gave yourself away. "WALSH," I said. "THIS FRIEND — WAS — IS — WAS — WAS A FRIEND."

"WHY WAS?"

"WALSH SAYS WE'VE STUCK TO EACH OTHER TOO MUCH. SAYS WE HAVE TO GET OUT AND MEET OTHER PEOPLE. WE'VE KNOWN EACH OTHER SINCE WE WERE TWELVE YEARS OLD."

"TELL WALSH YOU'RE DOING IT. YOU'VE MET ME! TRA-LA!"

Tra-la? Aha! "TRA-LA YOURSELF."

"ARE YOU LAFFING? I LIKE TO MAKE PEOPLE LAFF. DOES WALSH MAKE YOU LAFF?"

"SOMETIMES. MOSTLY, NO. A PRETTY SERIOUS PERSON."

That week I made a rule for myself. No talking about Julie to Top Hat. No thinking about Julie, no day-dreaming, no pretending things were going to work out. No Julie in the mind. I was going to think about something else. Other girls, food, Troy, Top Hat. . . . Think about avocados, anything at all but Julie. Thinking about her was like being sick, like being subjected to the Chinese water torture, like having a faucet dripping a drop at a time in my head.

On the radio, someone wailed, *"I just caa-aan't live without chewwww . . . my pore heart is breakin' an' blewwwww . . ."* My heart seemed fine, but the rest of me I wasn't so sure about. I started going to the gym every day after school and working out in the wrestling room, concentrating on all the basic moves. When I wrestled, I never thought about Julie.

And I talked to Top Hat a lot. That was my big distraction.

"BEAUTY PARLOR, I THINK YOU DRESS SORT OF QUIET AND CONSERVATIVE. IS THAT TRUE?"

"CLOSE ENOUGH. CHINOS AND MOCS."

"WE ARE VERY DIFFERENT! I'M ANYTHING BUT CON-SERVATIVE. WHICH IS A GOOD THING. FRIENDS SHOULD BE DIFFERENT. WHAT DO YOU LIKE TO DO IN YOUR SPARE TIME?"

"WRESTLING."

"QUIET, CONSERVATIVE, AND YOU LIKE WRESTLING?"

George you just blew it. How are we going to get out of this one?

"IF YOU EVER TRIED WRESTLING, YOU'D KNOW THERE'S NO FEELING SO GREAT AS GETTING YOUR OPPONENT PINNED."

"BEAUTY PARLOR, I DIDN'T KNOW GIRLS WRESTLED."

"YOU NEVER HEARD OF MUD WRESTLING?"

"I THOUGHT IT WAS A BIG SHOWBOAT. IS THAT WHAT YOU DO?"

"NO. THE REAL STUFF."

"WHERE?"

"AT MY SCHOOL." George, how long can you keep this going? It was like juggling. First I had two oranges in the air, now I had three.

"DO MANY GIRLS GO OUT FOR WRESTLING IN YOUR SCHOOL?"

"NO."

"YOU'RE A PIONEER."

"NOT REALLY."

"YOU'RE MODEST, BEAUTY PARLOR."

"NOT REALLY."

"YOU'RE STRONG. ANYBODY WHO WRESTLES HAS TO BE STRONG."

"THIS IS TRUE."

"I'D LIKE TO TRY MUD WRESTLING. WALLOW AROUND LIKE A PIG IN A BIG WET MUDPIE. SOUNDS LIKE FUN. I'LL TRY ANYTHING ONCE. WELL, MOST ANYTHING. . . . DID YOU EVER ENTER A WET T-SHIRT CONTEST?"

"NO!"

"WOULD YOU?"

"I'M NOT BUILT FOR IT." Here it is, George. The big question. "DID YOU EVER ENTER A WET T-SHIRT CONTEST, TOP HAT?"

"HATE TO ADMIT IT, BUT . . . YES. AND I WON."

Chapter 12

The Cliffside Growlers, our girls' basketball team, was playing the Greenfield Panthers for the county championship. "I'm going," Troy said. "You want to come?"

Greenfield was Julie's school. I figured it all out in a moment: I'd ask Julie to go — no date, just a friendly foursome. Afterward, we'd all go out for food. Julie and I would be together, but with other people. Wasn't that at least half of what she wanted? She'd always liked Troy; I remember once she'd said he had an interesting mind. *Interesting.* One of Julie's favorite words. I saw the four of us afterward in Troy's truck. They'd be talking and I'd sit back, putting in a remark here and there, idly playing with Julie's fingers. She'd see that we could do things with other people and still be together.

I phoned Julie. Beth answered. "Doesn't Julie ever answer the phone?" I said.

"You're lucky you got me, George. Make it fast. I'm getting ready to go out. If he ever shows up."

"Where is Julie this time?"

"She's out with Martin."

"Who?"

"Cousin Martin from Rockport, Mass."

"I didn't know she had a cousin in Rockport."

"Yes, George, she has a cousin in Rockport and so do I."

And did she have a cousin in Brockport and Hyannisport, Eelport, and Airport? "Tell her to call me when she comes in."

"Will do."

The minute I hung up, I called again. "Beth, do you give Julie my messages?"

"George, I do. Every time."

"I wish you hadn't said that."

"Listen, George, could I say something? This is serious. No jokes. I'm four years older than you, and I've had things happen to me."

"No, Beth. Don't say it. I know what you're going to say."

"George, really, it hurts me to see you like this."

"Right. Thanks." I hung up. I didn't want her pity. Ridicule me, despise me, but don't feel sorry for me.

That was Thursday. Friday I called Julie around five o'clock when I knew the whole family was home. It was masochistic. I had promised myself I wouldn't do it. But I didn't know when to quit.

"George?" her mother said. "Julie just ran out to the store for me. She ought to be back in ten minutes."

"Ten minutes?"

"That's right."

"Do you know if she's going to be home tonight?"

"No, I'm not sure what her plans are."

I hung up and started waiting again. Waiting is hell itself. Waiting for a phone call that, in your heart, you know is never going to come. I told everyone to keep off the phone. I set the timer and paced up and down, listening to it tick off the seconds. When it rang at ten minutes, I got an itch down my back imagining that Julie had just walked into her apartment. Okay, now her mother was giving her the message. *George called ten minutes ago. Call him back.*

I set the timer again. I'd give her another ten minutes. . . . *Bong!* Right. Here we go. Julie has just walked in. . . . *George called.* . . . She goes straight to the phone. . . . Or is it straight to the bathroom? *I'm sorry, George, she's not available.* . . .

I whipped through the house, checking to make sure the phones were all on the hook, testing each one for a dial tone. I paced the house like a lion guarding its young. If anyone made a move to a phone, I growled. There was the phone and modem in my sister's room, a Princess phone in my parents' room, a wall phone in the kitchen, the old-fashioned two-piece phone in the living room, the really old one in the basement. We even had a goddamn phone in the garage. When the phone rang in our house, you went into instant destruct. Your hair went straight up and your fingers stiffened, and you went, *"Yaaawwwww!"*

"What time are we going to the game?" Joanne said, looking up from her computer.

"What's with the 'we' stuff?"

"Mom said you should take me. Didn't you hear her?"

93

"No. You want to come?"

She shrugged. "Maybe."

"Okay, but you got to be ready on time."

"George! Look at this!" She pointed to the computer screen. "TOP HAT CALLING BEAUTY PARLOR."

I sat down at the terminal. "It's for me."

"Who's Top Hat?"

"A dressy dude."

"What's a dressy dude want to talk to you for?"

I pointed to the door. "Go."

"You're kicking me out of my own room?"

"You want to go to the game?" As soon as she left, I typed.

"BEAUTY PARLOR HERE. HELLO, TOP HAT."

"OH, I'M SO GLAD I GOT YOU. CAN YOU TALK?"

"I'M GOING OUT SOON, BUT I HAVE A FEW MINUTES. I'M WAITING FOR SOMEONE TO CALL ME."

"SOMEONE IMPORTANT?"

"RIGHT. THE MOST IMPORTANT PERSON IN MY LIFE."

"LUCKY YOU."

George, why is she sitting home alone? A girl who's five feet eleven-and-a-half and dances and enters wet T-shirt contests?

"LUCKY ME, TOP HAT, BUT ONLY IF THE SOMEONE IMPORTANT CALLS."

"OH, HE WILL! WHICH ONE IS IT? PIANO PLAYER?"

"NO. WALSH." As soon as I typed it, I was convinced that Julie was trying to get through, and as I thought it, every phone in the house started ringing.

"TOP HAT, SORRY, NO MORE TIME. THAT'S MY CALL."

I picked up the phone. "Hello, Julie, hold on a second."

"TALK TO YOU TOMORROW, TOP HAT."

"Julie? Troy is going to be here soon. We can swing

by and pick you up and we'll all go to the game at — "

"George. This is Troy. I'm leaving right now."

"Okay." That was that. Julie wasn't calling.

Joanne and I were outside when Troy drove up. "Hi, Troy," she said. "I'm going to the game with you." She looked pretty — her straight black eyebrows, her lips, her burning cheeks. You'd never guess that she spent half her life in front of the computer.

Troy pointed at me. "Do we have to take him, too?" He winked. "You want to be my girlfriend?"

Joanne's cheeks got even redder. "Thank you for not patronizing me," she said furiously. She pushed past me, went into the house, and slammed the door.

I got into the truck. "She'll never come out now. Let's go."

"What happened to her?"

"For a smart guy, you can be awfully dumb sometimes. One thing about Joanne, she hates anybody kiddy-talking her."

"I was just teasing. I didn't mean anything."

"You were flirting with her."

"I don't flirt. Girls flirt."

"Tell me about it."

At the gym, Troy and I stood up when the Panthers came out. They all looked leggy and tall. We gave them a little cheer. They were girls, weren't they?

Then our team came out, wearing red knee guards and red-and-white shirts. Troy slapped his big mitts together. Chris jogged by, biting her lip. Troy knew all the girls on the team. "Take it to the hoop, Chris," he yelled. "Dunk it, Paulette. . . . Come on, that was a foul," he yelled at the referee. "Denise was fouled."

95

Our Growlers were scrappy, fast, and tough. They went to the floor for the ball and crashed to the boards. The Greenfield Panthers had the height, though, and a lead at halftime. Troy went off to talk to someone. I stood up to stretch. That's when I saw Julie coming into the gym with a guy who had red hair tied back in a ponytail. I felt as if someone had grabbed me by the throat.

Julie and the redhead sat down on the other side of the court. I watched them leaning toward each other, smiling. Was that Rockport? Her cousin? When I'd heard *cousin*, I'd thought of someone younger, somebody with glasses maybe, some little overweight kid from the shore at Rockport.

The game started again, but I didn't know what was happening. I didn't see anything. After about ten minutes I walked over to where Julie and Rockport were sitting.

Julie, let's start all over again. Let it be as if we never met. A new story. It'll go like this: One day I saw you walking into an apartment building. Let it be the day I climbed the fire escape and saw you through the window. And let it be that I didn't know your name, and I went down and read your name on the mailbox. And let it be that you came along and saw me and invited me up to the house. And your family was there, and it was awkward. We didn't know what to say to each other. But when I left, we both knew it wasn't an ending. And let it be that I started calling you and you called me and we talked and we liked each other more and more. And let it be that we saw each other at this basketball game and I came over and sat with you. . . .

"Oh, hi, George," Julie said. "Cheering for your team? You're losing."

Close up this way, I could see her cousin had pimples. Lots of them. Still, he looked pretty confident, like somebody who thought about cleaning up the environment.

"George, this is my cousin, Martin Herlahan. He's from out of state."

"Boston," he said, putting out his hand.

I looked at his hand, I looked at him. I didn't like his face, I didn't like the way he talked or the color of his hair or the way he shook my hand. I sat down on the other side of Julie. "Keep your eye on Chris."

"Who's that?" her cousin said.

"Chris Roth," Julie said. "She's number ten." Then, to me, "We drove all over Clifton Heights today in Martin's car."

He leaned across Julie, smiling. "That took all of five minutes. No, I'm kidding. This is a really exciting burg."

Sarcastic bastard. What if I said, *Take a walk for yourself, this is my girl and I don't want you hanging around her. Even if you are her cousin from Rockport. Which I don't believe for a second.*

"But you really like it, Martin," Julie said. "Come on, admit it, you think Clifton has charm."

"Proletarian charm," he agreed.

They exchanged smiles.

Rockport started talking about Boston, what a great city it was and the great things you could do there and the great fishing in the Atlantic Ocean. And Julie was lapping it all up, as if we weren't across the river from New York and didn't have the greatest fishing and the greatest everything in the world right here.

"Julie," I said, interrupting something about all the concerts you could go to in Boston, "remember the

97

hayride we went on the year we were in eighth grade?"

"What about it?"

"Remember Pink Rabbit? Every time I went to your house she had fits."

"How could I forget her? She still lives there. What's the point, George?"

"Remember the tree house, Julie? Remember the time we went to the midnight movie?"

"Of course!"

"Who's Pink Rabbit?" Martin asked.

"A busybody who lives in our house."

Remember kissing, Julie? Remember taking off your shirt? Remember the way we loved each other?

I sat with my elbows on my knees, staring at the game. On a time-out, I stood up, stepped in front of Julie, stepped on Rockport's Nikes, and left.

I made my way out behind the stands. I was acutely aware of the game, the bouncing ball, the squeaking shuffle of feet across the floor, the calls and cries of the crowd. And I was aware of myself, the wounded warrior holding himself bravely upright.

I walked down a corridor. Green walls. A hall monitor's chair. Suddenly I had an image of Julie's cousin putting his hand on her knee. And I saw myself reaching over, slapping his hand away, and saying, *Cousins keep their roaming hands to themselves!*

You slap the wall. You want to scream. You want to grab something and break it. You want to punch someone. And you can't do anything, because you're not that kind of person. So you punch the wall. It's block, it's brick, it's stone. You punch the wall again. It's iron and cement. You're hurting yourself and it feels good.

I found Troy's truck in the parking lot. The doors

to the cab were locked. I climbed into the box. The sky was dark. I heard the referees' whistles from the gym, the blare of the band. My knuckles burned. I lay down and fell asleep.

A movement of the car woke me, then voices and sounds. I sat up. Troy and Chris were in front. I rapped on the window. "Hey, guys, I'm back here." I gave them a minute to pull themselves together. When I climbed in front, they both started to laugh. They were wearing their red team jackets. They made me think of a couple of kids in red pj's. "I thought you left," Troy said.

"I didn't mean to interrupt anything here."

"No sweat. Let's go get something to eat."

Everything was bright, loud, and crowded when we went into Staggs. It looked like everybody who'd been at the game was there. I had a hand on Chris's shoulder. We found a place over by the wall. "Let's split a pizza," I said. "How about a pitcher of beer?"

"Not me," Troy said. "You guys go ahead, but I'm driving."

I recognized some kids at the next table. "Hey, Patsy! Ralph, how's it going? Ginny, looking good."

Julie and her cousin walked in. "There's Julie," I said to Chris. "That's her cousin with her. That's her story, anyway." I was talking too much. I stood up. "Julie, over here," I yelled. "You guys like pizza? Come on, we've been waiting for you."

Julie started to protest. I found a couple of chairs and pushed them to our table. "Sit down, Marian. Marian and Martin, meet Chris and Troy. Marian and Martin are cousins," I explained. "You don't see the resemblance?" I took Julie's chin and turned her head.

Julie shook me off. "George, you're being obnoxious." She looked across at Chris. "Hi, I'm Julie Walsh. We met once, remember? I thought you played a great game."

"Thanks," Chris said. "I was only two for eight from the foul line."

I jumped up and started serving them pizza. "One for you, Maid Marian." I gave her my plate. "*And* one for you!" I slapped a slice of pizza, cheese side down, into Martin's hand,

"George!" Julie looked furious.

"Sorry. Sorry, sorry, sorry." I handed him a bunch of napkins. "Sorry, old Rocksport."

"You want to leave?" Julie asked him.

"No, that's fine. If your friend here can restrain himself — "

"Oh, he can restrain himself, if he wants to," Julie said.

I sat back and nursed my beer. I was impressed with my restraint. Here was Cousin Martin right across from me, and the worst thing I'd done was give him a little cheese in the wrong place. I was remarkable. I was letting him live. I felt generous to an unbelievable degree.

"Hey, Marian, remember those afternoons in the apartment? One time her sister came in on us and caught us. You know what sly dog Beth did? She panted. Panted like a dog!" I pushed the pitcher of beer across the table. It sloshed toward him. "Drink up, Martin. Slurp it up. Don't waste it. Maid Marian doesn't like beer, but I can tell you do." I admired my cleverness.

Then I started beaming mental messages to Julie. *Julie, do you see me? Look up. Look out of the window*

100

of your eyes. Princess Julie. Maid Marian. I'm down here in the dust, waiting for you to recognize me. Hello, hello. Are you there? Are you home? What are you thinking about? Martin? Is he calling you, too? Are you aching to kiss Mr. Martin's pimply face? Are you getting all excited by Señor Martin's deep voice and smart talk? Where are you going when you leave here? Driving away in his car?

The thought of Julie in Martin's car, in Martin's arms, made me writhe and burn. I got so hot I couldn't sit still. The seat burned under me. I leaped up from the chair. "Julie!" I was on the George Washington Bridge again scrawling her name in Magic-Glo. *George loves Julie forever and ever and ever.* I leaped into the air. "Julie!" A couple of kids in the next booth stood up and looked at me. They recognized a psycho when they saw one. "Julie! Julio!" I howled. "Juuuuuuulissimo!"

When I looked again she was gone. "Where is she? Where's Julie?"

"Gone. Sit down, George," Troy said. "You're drunk."

Driving home, Chris held my hand. "I feel sorry for you, George. I know you're acting like this because of you and Julie breaking up."

At my house, Troy got out with me. "You okay?"

"Give me a cigarette," I said. He lit a cigarette for me. I took a couple of puffs.

"You're going to be all right," Troy said. "Don't take it so hard." He patted my shoulder.

"Good friend," I said.

"She'll come around. You'll see."

I threw the cigarette down. I didn't want to be around him anymore. When you're miserable, you don't

101

want to be around successful people. They're stupid because they think everyone else can be as happy as they are.

I went inside. Everyone was asleep. I sat in the kitchen and slowly chewed a leftover chicken leg. I stared at the second hand on the clock. Would Julie call me? Had she said she'd call me? I tried to remember. Call me tomorrow, I'd told her. Was it now or was it tomorrow? I squinted at the clock and decided it was tomorrow. Which meant I could call her. I sat on the counter and chewed and dialed her number.

The phone rang once. Twice. Three times. "Hello, hello," I said. It rang again.

"What?" someone said. It was Beth.

"Julie?"

"Who is this?"

"Who is *that*? *This* is George calling Julie. Over."

"George! Do you know what time it is?"

"George calling Julie. Over."

"George, your voice sounds funny. Are you bombed?"

"Is Maid Marian there? Over. Is Martin there? Over."

"George, hang up and don't call again. Nobody's going to like you if you do."

Beth hung up. I went upstairs. The night-lights along the baseboard threw up a yellow glow. I steadied myself against the wall. A red eye gleamed from my sister's room. She was asleep with her head under the pillow. I went in and sat down in front of the red eye. "Hello, computer," I mumbled. I started typing.

"DEAR TOP HAT. THE PERSON I CARE ABLOUT MOST IN THE WORLD HS DITCHED ME AND I'M FEELINGMISERABLE. MN SORRY TO TO DO THIS TO YEOU, DON'T HAVE TO ANSWER THATS OKAY.

"DEAR ICEBOX, I DONT KNOW IF YOU'VE EVER HAD

102

THIS HAPPEN TO YOU, BEING DITCHED, DUMPED, DIS-CARDED. THE THREE TERRIBLE D'S. DITCHED, DUMPED, AND DISCARDED. I FEEL LIKE A CARTON, TORN OPEN, EMPTIED OUT, KICKED ASIDE. YOU KNOW WHAT, TOP-BOX, LOVE IS DUMB. WHEN YOU LOVE SOMEONE YOU'RE NOT SMART. I'M NOT SMART.

"HOW ABOUT THIS, ICEHAT, THIS IS BRILLIANT AND EXPLAINSIT ALL. LOVE IS A FALL. FREEFALL WITH NO GRABONS, NO QUICK EXITS. WHEN IT FLIES IT'S ITS FAN-TASTIC. BUT WHEN IT FALLS WHEN YOU FALL AND CRASHES IT'S IT'S . . . I CAN'T TELL YOU WHAT IT IS . . . IT'S SO BAD I CAN'T EVEN SAY IT. AND ANYWAY I'M SLOSHED.

"I DON'T UNDERSTAND IT. DON'T UNDERSTAND.

"I HOPE THIS NEVER HAPPENS TO YOU."

I sat there for a while, staring at the screen. Then I erased everything and went down the hall to my room.

Chapter 13

"Wake up, wake up. Come on, open those eyes."

I stared through gummy lashes, then sat up, thrashing aside the covers. Something with wild red hair and hot round eyes like Little Orphan Annie dug a finger into my chest. "Joanne?" I blinked at her. "What the hell . . . ?" My mouth was dry, my stomach roiled around like soup.

"What's the matter with you?" She sat down on the edge of the bed and pulled off the red wig.

"Don't ever drink." I could barely lift my head.

"You got bombed? George, you're stupid. What do you feel like?"

"Like my brains are spilling out of my ears."

"Are you sick?"

"Sick and sorry," I said hoarsely, trying to remember last night and what I did.

"Want me to tell her to call back?"

"Who?"

"You've got a phone call. It's Julie."

"Why didn't you tell me?" I staggered to my feet, and almost fell. I had to take small careful steps. Sudden movements made the liquid in my head rush to one side and then the other.

Julie calling me? There was something wrong with that. It should have been right, but I knew it was wrong. Some profound problem existed if Julie was calling me. Some awful question. . . .

"Julie?" I licked my lips. "What time is it?"

"One o'clock in the afternoon. Why did you call me last night? Do you know you woke my father and my mother and my sister? That was incredibly inconsiderate."

"I'm sorry."

"What did you have to say to me that couldn't wait?"

"I don't remember."

"You *don't remember*? You wake up the whole house and you can't do any better than that?"

"I wanted to sing you a song. Is that nicer? Does that make you happy, Julie?"

"George, what's the problem? You act like you're going over the edge. Last night — "

"What'd I do last night? I wasn't responsible. Whatever it was, I'm sorry."

"George. . . ." She sighed.

"Julie, I love you. Doesn't that mean anything to you? You don't even talk to me anymore."

"I thought that was all settled."

"What? What was settled? Nothing was settled."

"Damn it, George. . . ."

I listened hopefully to her sighs of impatience as if

105

they were signs of renewed love. "Let's meet, Julie, let's take a walk. We'll talk and — "

"We don't have that much to talk about."

"Yes, we do," I said insistently. "I want to talk to you. Meet me on Cliff Boulevard right now."

There was silence for a moment. Then she said quietly, "All right, Cliff Boulevard in an hour. Our regular place by the post office."

I loved the way she said that. *Our regular place.* I took a cold shower, put on a pair of clean chinos, combed my hair, and ran downstairs. My mother was waiting for me.

"What time did you come in last night, George?"

"Not late."

"Does that mean it was early in the morning?"

"Not that late!"

"What time?"

"I didn't look, Ma."

"How convenient for you, sweetheart. What were you doing?"

"Oh . . . nothing much. Out with Troy and Chris. . . . Pizza . . . you know. . . ." Questioned closely, I was vague. Facts are meat for parents. They're like lions at the kill. The more facts they have, the more ferociously they growl.

"You were drinking."

"Well . . . I was having fun, Mom."

"George, what sensible person would poison themselves for the fun of it? It's like jumping off a ten-story building to look brave."

"I know, Mom. I'm off it, believe me."

"If you could see yourself now. . . . You look like you just climbed out of the popcorn machine. Sit down, I'm going to give you some breakfast."

I wasn't hungry, but I downed the orange juice, made a sandwich of the bread, took an apple, and ran all the way to Cliff Boulevard. It helped clear my head.

Julie was waiting for me. She had her hands in her jacket pockets, a white knit cap on her head. "Apple." I presented it to her. We walked along for a while, not saying much. She ate the apple and once gave me a tiny, rueful smile. "So much urgency to see me, George. What was it all about?"

"Just . . . urgency to see you, Julie. . . . Who was that guy you were with last night?"

"Martin? My cousin? What do you mean, who was he?"

"He didn't act like a cousin."

"How's a cousin supposed to act?"

"Not so interested."

"What do you mean, *interested*?"

"I saw the looks he was giving you, the way he got his hand on your leg — "

"You're crazy!"

"He probably has a knee fetish," I said gloomily. "Any excuse and he was pawing your knees."

"What's the matter with you, George? I like Martin. He's my cousin. He's led an interesting life. You know what he did the summer he was sixteen? He biked from Boston to Spokane."

"Fascinating."

"You're jealous of my cousin. That's unbelievable."

"What's more unbelievable is that he is, in fact and actually, your cousin," I said. I spoke carefully, pronouncing every word fully.

There was a spark in her eyes, a flash. "Do you think I'm lying to you?"

"Lying? Did I say it, Julie? No, I wouldn't say that.

107

But just tell me this. All the years I knew you and I never heard about him before. How can that be?"

"How can that be?" she mimicked angrily. "Do you ever hear anything except what concerns George Farina?"

I wanted to say something sharp and dry and bright. Something to show her that she was wrong about me.

"I've talked about Martin before," she said. "Believe me, George, I've talked about him. He's not a deep, dark secret in our family."

"Why'd you write me that letter?" I said.

"George, that was weeks ago."

"It doesn't feel that way to me."

"So that's what this is all about. You still haven't accepted what I said — "

"Julie, how perceptive!"

"I don't know why I even agreed to meet you," she said.

"Why *did* you?" the fool asked. Hoping she'd say, *Because I love you, George.*

"Because you're so impossibly persistent! And because you are George, and I do love you, and we were together so long, and it's just *hard* on me to keep saying no to you! Why do I have to keep turning you down? George, listen to me. Try to hear this. I'm opening a door for us. For me. For you. A door to walk out of. This is a chance for both of us to find things out. We were in one small room too long." She stopped and took me by the arm. "George, can you hear me? The door is open."

"Julie, can you hear *me*? I don't give a damn about your eff-ing door. Slam it! Shut it! Come on back into that room with me."

108

"No." She stepped away, put her hand to her throat. "Just talking about it chokes me."

"Was that what it was like for you all the time we were going together? You felt strangled?"

"I loved you," she said. "You know that. And I still love you, but — "

I tuned out. I knew what she was going to say. I didn't want to hear it again. I dug into my pockets, looking for a cigarette, a toothpick, a stick of gum — anything to chew on. I turned my pockets inside out, emptied out the lint, a few pennies, keys, and a dollar bill. Dumped it all out on the sidewalk. "It's cleaning day," I said.

Julie stared. "Well, I think I ought to go now."

"Right. Me, too." I picked up my keys, left everything else. "I've got a lot of stuff to do."

"George — " She held out her hand, as if to say, "peace."

I slapped it, flat-fived it hard. "See you around, man." I walked away.

Chapter 14

"I'M SEVENTEEN YEARS OLD. I LEFT HOME LAST YEAR AND WENT TO LIVE WITH MY FATHER. I'M NOT A RUN-AWAY, MORE A THROWAWAY."

Throwaway? A little dramatic, wouldn't you say, George?

"I THOUGHT YOU WERE OLDER. I'M SEVENTEEN, TOO."

"THAT'S AMAZING. TWO GIRLS WHO DON'T KNOW EACH OTHER, AND WE TURN OUT TO BE SO COMPATIBLE AND THE SAME AGE. DON'T TELL ME YOU LEFT HOME, TOO?"

"NO. I'VE GOT TWO PARENTS AND A SISTER."

"I WOULD NEVER HAVE LEFT HOME, EITHER, BUT I COULDN'T GET ALONG WITH MY STEPFATHER, AND MY MOTHER DIDN'T STAND UP FOR ME. SHE KNEW HOW I LOVED DANCING. SHE WAS A DANCER IN NEW YORK ONCE. THAT'S WHERE SHE MET MY FATHER. MY GRAND-MOTHER WAS A MARATHON DANCER."

"MY PARENTS NEVER DID ANYTHING INTERESTING LIKE THAT."

"I USED TO CLIMB OUT THE WINDOW AT NIGHT WHEN I WAS FIFTEEN AND RIDE OUT TO A CLUB OUTSIDE OF TOWN. IT WAS REALLY A BAR, BUT IT HAD A LITTLE STAGE WITH A SPOTLIGHT. I WASN'T DOING ANYTHING BAD. I WAS DANCING. I HAD A SPECIAL COSTUME I WORE. IT WAS SKIMPY, BUT NO WORSE THAN A LOT OF BIKINIS.

"BUT WHEN MY STEPFATHER FOUND OUT, HE WENT NUTS. HE DRAGGED ME OUT OF THERE AND AFTER THAT I WAS FORBIDDEN TO GO OUT, FORBIDDEN TO LOCK MY DOOR. I COULDN'T EVEN HAVE A PHONE CALL IN PRI-VATE."

What do you think, George? Is she telling us a story? Fifteen and dancing in a bar?

"WHERE DO YOU GO TO SCHOOL?" That's good, George, dig for the facts.

"IN NEW YORK THERE'S ONLY ONE PLACE, THE SCHOOL FOR THE PERFORMING ARTS. BUT I DIDN'T MAKE IT. I DON'T WANT TO TALK ABOUT THE SCHOOL I'M IN. IT'S NOTHING. IT'S A PLACE TO GO. I'M JUST GOING TO FINISH AND GET OUT. EVER SINCE SIXTH GRADE, I'VE BEEN ASKING MYSELF WHY I HAVE TO SIT IN CLASSES AND LEARN THINGS LIKE ALGEBRA AND HISTORY THAT WILL NEVER MEAN ANYTHING TO ME. I'M A DANCER. I DANCE. I HAVE TO DANCE. I LOVE ALL KINDS OF DANCING. I EVEN DO BELLY DANCING WITH A JEWEL IN MY BELLY BUTTON."

I sat there, getting warm, imagining Top Hat, who entered wet T-shirt contests, this tall, gorgeous dancer, weaving her arms around, flashing a big diamond in her navel.

What about that, Julie. We never talked about belly buttons.

111

"BEAUTY PARLOR, DOES YOUR BELLY BUTTON POP IN
OR OUT? MINE GOES IN. IF IT WENT OUT, I'D BE OUT
OF LUCK. NO JEWELS. HOW ABOUT YOU?"

"WAIT A MINUTE," I said. "I HAVE TO LOOK. . . .
IN."

"WELL, THAT'S A RELIEF, ISN'T IT? YOU COULD BELLY
DANCE, TOO."

"I'M NOT THE ARTISTIC TYPE."

"I BET YOU'RE NOT ORDINARY, THOUGH."

That was a nice thing to say. "I MIGHT START WORK-
ING WITH WOOD. REFINISHING OLD PIECES OF FURNI-
TURE. I'M WAITING TO HEAR ABOUT A JOB."

"I BUILT A SET OF BOOKCASES FOR MY FATHER."

I thought, Is there anything she hasn't done?

I kept looking for mistakes in Top Hat's stories, for
contradictions, for the places where she said one thing
one time and another the next time. I asked her a lot
of questions. I admit I was a little suspicious. She told
me so many things about herself, things she didn't
have to tell me, things a careful person wouldn't say.
We called ourselves friends, and in one way we were
very close, but in another way we hardly knew each
other. It was the effect of the computer. We didn't
even know each other's names. And she had the most
basic thing about me wrong, my gender.

Every time I talked to her, I was tempted to tell her
the truth. It was in my mind. *Top Hat, I've been putting
you on, playing a trick on you. I'm not Beauty Parlor.
I'm not a girl. I'm just plain male — boy — me.*

Sometimes, I felt like a spy in a foreign country.
The Top Hat Nation. The Nation of Girls. Under-
cover agent, U.S. Male, with nobody to send a post-
card to. *Having a wonderful time. Learning new things*

112

every day. Wish you were here. On second thought,
wish I was there . . . with her.

"WHAT DOES YOUR FATHER SAY ABOUT YOUR DANC-
ING?"

"MY FATHER LOVES MY DANCING. HE'S A JOURNALIST,
BUT HE HAS THE RUSSIAN SOUL. EVEN WHEN SHE DI-
VORCED HIM, MY MOTHER SAID HE WAS THE MOST BEAU-
TIFUL MAN SHE EVER KNEW."

"THEN WHY DID SHE DIVORCE HIM?"

"BECAUSE HE WAS NEVER AROUND. HE'D THINK OF
SOMETHING AND HE'D GO, DISAPPEAR, FORGET HER,
FORGET US, FORGET EVERYTHING. IT UNNERVED HER;
SHE WANTED A MAN WHO KNEW HE HAD A FAMILY. IT
WASN'T THAT HE DIDN'T LOVE US. IT WAS JUST THAT
WHEN HE GETS AN IDEA FOR AN ARTICLE, HE GETS
EXCITED AND FORGETS EVERYTHING ELSE. NOW MY
MOTHER HAS MY STEPFATHER, WHO DOESN'T LET HER
TAKE A STEP WITHOUT ASKING HIM FIRST. I'M LIKE MY
FATHER. THAT'S WHY I COULDN'T LIVE IN CHAMPION."

"DOES HE HAVE TO DO A LOT OF RESEARCH?"

"SOMETIMES HE CAN DO IT RIGHT HERE, BUT A LOT
OF TIMES HE HAS TO TRAVEL. HE WAS IN SACRAMENTO
LAST MONTH DOING RESEARCH ON GOLD MINING. AND
THEN HE DID SOME WORK ON THE PRIMATE RESEARCH
THEY'RE DOING AT THE SAN DIEGO ZOO. HE MAY WORK
THAT INTO A BOOK HE WANTS TO DO."

"HOW LONG WAS HE GONE?"

"OH, I DON'T KNOW, TWO WEEKS. THAT'S ABOUT THE
LONGEST HE EVER STAYS AWAY."

I tried to think of the times my parents had left me.
A day or two. Maybe once or twice they went away
on a vacation. But when I thought about it, I realized
I'd never been alone. There was always somebody there,

113

my sister, the baby-sitter, one of my grandparents.

"DO YOU MIND BEING ALONE?"

"I'M USED TO BEING ALONE. I DON'T LOVE IT, BUT MY FATHER CALLS A LOT. . . . DID I TELL YOU I DANCED ON SATURDAY? IT WAS A FANTASTIC DAY. I PERFORMED AT THE EDGE OF CENTRAL PARK, NEAR THE PLAZA HOTEL. DO YOU KNOW THAT PLACE NEAR THE TOY STORE?"

"SORT OF." I tried to imagine her dancing and people walking by, some of them stopping to watch.

"I WORE MY TUXEDO AND TOP HAT, AND I DANCED ALONG THE LIP OF THE FOUNTAIN. MY DANCING WAS GOOD. SOME DAYS THE SPIRIT PASSES ME BY. SOME DAYS IT COMES TO REST WITH ME."

"WELL, I'M GLAD THE SPIRIT DROPPED IN."

"PEOPLE ALWAYS LAUGH WHEN I SAY SOMETHING LIKE THAT. DOES THE SPIRIT EVER VISIT YOU?"

"I'M NOT THE SPIRITUAL TYPE."

"I THINK YOU'RE MORE SPIRITUAL THAN YOU GIVE YOURSELF CREDIT FOR. I CAN TELL YOU HAVE A BEAUTIFUL SOUL."

"George. George, I'm talking to you. George!" My sister's voice yanked me back into reality. "George, if you wouldn't mind, that's my computer and I'd like to log a little time on it."

"TOP HAT, MY JAILER IS HERE. GOTTA GO."

"TALK TO YOU TOMORROW, BEAUTY PARLOR."

One day Top Hat asked me if I was alone.

And I asked back if she meant alone like the way she was alone when her father took off on an assignment.

"NO, I MEANT ALONE, REGARDING FRIENDS."

"I HAVE FRIENDS."

"WE ARE FRIENDS, AREN'T WE?"

114

"SURE." I thought so. I still thought it was a little strange being friends with a computer, but it was growing on me. 1. Top Hat was a distraction. (When I talked to her, I didn't think about Julie.) 2. She was a puzzle with lots of unanswered questions. (Unlike Julie, who was a puzzle with lots of questionable answers.) 3. She made me laugh. (While Julie could only make me cry.)

"BEAUTY PARLOR, WHAT'S YOUR REAL NAME?"

"WHY DO YOU WANT TO KNOW?"

"WE KNOW SO MUCH ABOUT EACH OTHER, WHY NOT?"

"WHY CHANGE THINGS?"

"THESE NAMES ARE SILLY. TOP HAT. BEAUTY PARLOR. I WANT TO KNOW YOUR REAL NAME."

"MY REAL NAME? MY REAL NAME IS — MY NAME IS GEORGE."

"GEORGE. I LIKE THAT. I KNEW A GIRL IN CHAMPION WHOSE NAME WAS MICHAEL. EVERYBODY CALLED HER MICKEY. AND ANOTHER GIRL WHOSE NAME WAS BERNIE. YOU'RE MY FIRST GEORGE. IS IT SHORT FOR GEORGIA?"

"JUST GEORGE . . . GEORGE ANDREW FARINA."

"GEORGE ANDREW!!!!!!!!!!!!!"

"THAT'S THE NAME MY FATHER WANTED FOR ME. WHAT ABOUT YOU? WHAT'S YOUR NAME?"

"ROSEMARY."

"ROSEMARY. A LOT NICER THAN ICEBOX."

Chapter 15

During the week, one of the tenants on the top floor in the apartment house called to complain that there was a leak in the roof. My father asked me to take care of it. "There's tar stored by the door to the roof, George."

I went over after school and gunked up a bunch of cracks. On the way down from the roof, I walked slowly by the Walshes' door, smelled potatoes and onions. My stomach started to growl. Was it hunger or love? I stood there for a moment. "Julie?"

Her father came up the stairs. He was coming from work, his boots white with dust.

"Hello, Mr. Walsh," I said.

"George." He nodded his head. He looked grim, prepared to subdue the overheated lover. "Looking for Julie?"

"No, I was just fixing the roof."

"Good. I heard they had some problems upstairs. Well, come on in. Julie's probably here." He put his hand on my shoulder and held it there as he walked me inside. "I wanted to talk to you. . . ."

Had he and his daughter worked this out together? Had they finally had enough of George and his *damned, persistent* phone calls? Was he going to grab me by the seat of my pants and pitch me out the window and over the cliff? Good-bye, George, this is the last time you disturb our house with your pleading, whining, silly, begging telephone calls!

We stood looking out in silence at the New York skyline. The sun was down and New York had begun to light up. Mr. Walsh opened the window and the sounds of the river and the highway rose up to us. "I like to stand here at night and look at the river and the lights," he said. "A quiet time, George. I need that at the end of the day."

Now he was getting to it. He needed quiet after working hard all day, and who was disturbing his peace and quiet? He had his arm around the problem. Any moment now, he was going to be rid of the problem once and for all.

"George, sometimes I stand here and feel how lucky I am to be on this side of the river and have this apartment and this view."

I heard sounds from the other rooms. Julie? In her room, avoiding me?

"I'd hate to lose this place," Mr. Walsh said.

"My father would never sell it," I said.

"That's what I want to hear. This is our home. We've lived here since we've been married. Now those damned developers are all over the cliffs." He pointed to the dark shape of the apartment towers that loomed up to the north and the south. "They've got us surrounded."

"Mr. Walsh? Did you say Julie was here?"

"Julie?" He knocked on her door. "Julie, you in there? There's someone to see you."

Julie came out of her bedroom and Mr. Walsh went down the hall. She had her hand up, shielding her eyes. I couldn't make out her expression. "It's me," I said.

"Oh. . . . Hi."

"How's everything?"

"Mmm. Fine."

"Well, your father invited me in."

"Did he?"

"We were just enjoying the view."

"Were you?"

The less she said, the more I said. "I was thinking of asking you something."

"Yes?"

"I thought we might go to a movie sometime this weekend. You like Michael J. Fox, we could go see that one."

"You don't really mean that."

"You're right, I don't." Why did I keep doing this to myself? "How about something wholesome then, like a chainsaw movie?" I heard someone cough in the other room. I looked over her shoulder. I saw legs crossed, half-laced boots. "Who's he?"

"A friend." Julie pulled the door shut. "What is it, George? What do you want?"

I stared at her. "Me? What do I want? Nothing, Julie," I said. "Nothing at all." And I walked out.

Chapter 16

"Hello. May I speak to George Farina?"

"Speaking."

"George, this is Lydia Joy, the village woodworker. It's taken me a while to get back to you. Are you still interested in working?"

"Well, sure."

"You sound a little hesitant?"

"No, I — "

"You certainly weren't hesitant the morning you asked me for a job."

She didn't give me a chance to catch my breath. "I'm interested."

"I want something definite. I don't have the time to waste on someone who's going to change his mind half an hour after he takes the job."

"I'm committed," I said, trying to put a little of her

crackle into my voice. "I want the job. I want to work on wood."

"Good. Can you come to work tomorrow?"

"Tomorrow? Saturday?"

"What's the problem?"

"No, no problem. I was just thinking — Okay, sure. Tomorrow." I wouldn't be able to work for my father, but that was okay.

"I can count on you? I open to the public at nine, but I'm there at eight, and I want you there then, too."

"Okay. No sweat. I'll be there at eight. And thanks."

"Don't thank me yet. Let's see if this is going to work out."

I hung up and whooped. And who do you think I thought to call? Julie? I called Troy instead.

His mother answered. "Oh, George, I'm giving a lesson now," she whispered, as if she were in a library.

"Sorry, Mrs. Bonner. I just want to talk to Troy for a few minutes."

"He's not home yet."

"Do you know where he is?"

"No," she whispered. "I'll tell him you called. I'm sorry, I have to hang up now. My lesson is waiting."

I started to dial Julie. I had to grab my hand and move it away. What would I say to her? Tell her about the job? Why? She wasn't interested. What was the point? Just to let her know that life *was* going on? That I wasn't dragging around, brooding over her?

I'd make it short and crisp. *Julie, this won't take long. I just want to tell you about this interesting and maybe important opportunity that's come my way.* That wasn't crisp. It was stuffy and pompous and boring.

I'm beginning to think of wood as a way of life, Julie.

Wood as a way of life? Right there, she'd probably start yawning.

My mind is working, Julie, clicking and clacking. Pushing you out of it has left a big, cool space for other things. I've begun to think you never knew the real me, Julie. I'm not just old reliable, ordinary George. I can do some surprising things . . . such as getting this new job. . . .

I told myself, *do not call her.* Turn down the heat. Don't make this phone call.

But the thought had crept in and I was like an alcoholic, a drug addict, a cigarette fiend. He knows he can't touch the stuff, and still he picks up the glass, he lights the cigarette. . . .

I picked up the phone. With every ring I expected to hear Julie's voice. That special hello with a little expectant lift at the end. The phone rang and rang. Eight . . . nine . . . ten . . . I hung up on seventeen, my age.

Five minutes later I called again. Beth answered. "I just walked in, George. What timing. How did you know?"

"I'm across the street watching the house."

"I wouldn't put it past you, George. I suppose you want to talk to Julie? She's not here, George. But even if she was. . . ." Beth sighed. "George. I don't know why you keep calling her."

"I have something to tell her, Beth."

"Listen, can I say something? Everyone here likes you and wishes — "

"Everyone, except Julie, Beth."

"No, that's not true. She likes you. It's only — you know Julie, once she makes up her mind. . . ."

"Understood."

"You're still saying that!"

121

"It bothers you, too?"

"No, it's just that Julie mentioned something about it, that she was doing it, too. I thought it was pretty funny."

"You know anything about wood, Beth?"

"Only that sometimes I think your head is made of it."

"Same old sweet Beth."

"George, you want me to give my sister a message?"

"Tell her I called to say hello. Tell her I don't think she has the guts to talk to me."

"Anything else?"

"Tell her I've taken a sharp turn in my life. I have a new career and a new friend."

"Understood."

"She hired you?" Troy said. "So you conned her into it."

"Bull, my man. I got this job on my outstanding merits and qualifications."

"Ah, so. What was that song and dance, 'I'm strong, Ms. Joy. I'll work hard, Ms. Joy.' Do you know what you're getting yourself into? Dragon Lady there will run your ass off and pay you pennies."

"I'm not doing it for the money."

"Then you're not even one quarter as sane as I thought you were. What're you doing it for?"

"Experience."

"Good luck. Think of me tomorrow while you're piling up experience. I'll be truckin' on up the Garden State to see the old man. He had to send me twenty bucks for gas."

"What are you going to do in Binghamton?" Troy's

father had just opened a restaurant. "Does your father want you up there to work?"

"Work? Sure, I'll work. But then we'll be moving. Dad and I are going to hit the high spots."

"In Binghamton? What kind of high spots would that be?"

"Use your imagination, old son. My father's a free man and so am I."

"What does Chris say about that?"

"Chris who?"

"Since when?"

"I had a little dust-up with the lady."

"What happened?"

"Who knows? She's too damn sensitive. I said something about her teeny-tiny brain, and she thought it was an insult. To be precise, I called her a birdbrain."

"What do you have between your ears? Why would you call her a birdbrain?"

"Teasing, teasing. You know me, big, bluff, affable me. Always saying things I don't mean. She's supposed to be able to read between the lines. I do it with you, don't I? If I called you a birdbrain, you'd be flattered."

"Yeah, well, coming from someone with half a brain — "

"There, you said it, but am I insulted? She said I didn't display enough feeling. I told her maybe it's because I'm Norwegian. Where we come from, it's so cold, you open your mouth too wide and you'll frostbite your tongue."

"Great theory. It must have gone over big with Chris."

"Forget it, George. Whose side are you on? Is it us against them or isn't it? I didn't mean anything by it.

It just slipped out and she took it seriously. I told her to do it to me, call me anything she wanted to. 'Go ahead,' I said. 'Don't hold back! Pound me! Hit me in that blubber!' It just made her madder. You ever get into that stuff with Julie? No, you didn't. You tiptoed around her, right? You didn't make it dangerous for yourself. . . . Why don't you call Chris? Maybe she's desperate enough to go out with you."

"I don't feel like seeing anybody."

"Still carrying the torch for Julie?"

"Julie who?"

"You're working someplace else?" My father took it personally. Just what I'd been afraid of. "What am I going to do today without you?"

"Dad." I'd made the mistake of waiting till the last minute to tell him. "You can get somebody else to sweep the floor. What's the big deal if I'm at Leonard's or not?"

"The big deal, my son, is that it's a family business and you're part of the family. People expect to see you. They feel good when they see you. Don't you feel any sense of responsibility?"

"Pop. . . ." He was giving me looks, a lot of wrinkled forehead and darting eyebrow. He was packing all this negative energy, piling me hip-high in guilt. "You're cutting me down, Dad. Making me feel guilty as hell."

"What are you going to do about it?"

"I told her I was coming in."

"You can tell her you were mistaken, and you're not coming."

"You don't really want me to do that, do you?"

My father lit a cigarette. "George, you do what you think is right."

124

"Dad — " I glanced at the clock. "I'm sorry. . . . Can I take the car?"

He gave me an incredulous look. "Absolutely not. Not coming to work and you want my car?" He puffed furiously. "You have nerve, I'll say that for you. And how am I supposed to get to work?"

"You just have to call the shop and somebody'll come for you. Do you want me to bike seven miles?"

"You're young and strong. You don't smoke, your lungs are fine."

"I'm going to Englewood. I'll be biking through heavy traffic. It means nothing to you, even if I kill myself?"

"No comment, my son."

After that, I had no time for anything. I grabbed a donut and ate it as I pedaled to Lydia Joy's. I was half an hour late. "Sorry," I said. "I thought I'd have a car."

She studied me for so long I had the uneasy feeling that my face was covered with white sugar. I took a swipe at my mouth.

"I fired you already."

"Oh, no! I haven't even started working! That's not fair." I wanted this job. "I know I'm supposed to be here at eight. I won't be late again. I know you can use me." I made a muscle. "I have them on both arms."

She almost smiled. It was okay. She was going to give me a try.

She started me off sweeping. Wouldn't you know? My luck. I might as well have been in Leonard's. At least there were people to talk to there. Lydia Joy wasn't a talker. All morning, she was either on the phone or working in back on furniture. I swept, moved things around, ran out once to buy her a sandwich.

After lunch, she finally gave me some real work,

removing paint on a Boston rocker. "I want every little bit and speck of that paint gone."

"Will do." I went to work, attacking each blemish like an enemy. Loosen the old paint up with the remover, scrape, smooth, attack the next blemish. It was like popping zits. Toward the end of the day Lydia Joy came over to inspect my work and show me where I needed to sand some more.

"I do everything by hand. I never dip furniture to remove the old finish because it ruins the wood." She blew dust off the chair. "Here's the stuff we use," she said pulling a can off a shelf. "It soaks into the wood. It revives it, brings out the natural grain and color." She ran her hand over the seat of the chair. "You see how it is?" she said. "There's something old and fine here that a new piece can never have." Then she asked me to work again the next day.

"Sunday?"

"Eight o'clock."

"I'll be here."

Biking home, my arms felt as heavy as the wood I'd been working on, and the ride seemed more like seventy miles. But I liked the dryness of my hands and the smell of wood and linseed oil that rode with me.

In the morning, everyone was asleep when I got up. I grabbed some food and got out my bike. The streets were wet. It had rained during the night. When I'd told my mother I was working today, she'd said, "Sunday, George? Why? You don't have to do that." All I did was smile and shake my head.

That day Lydia Joy had me take the old finish off a small commode. There were several layers of paint on it, starting with black and then green and getting down to a stubborn white glaze that resisted me all day. I worked steadily, hardly stopping.

The commode was square and sturdy, as ready for use as it must have been the day it was built. It had been made by human hands, not machines. Removing the finish, I'd had a chance to examine the drawer joinings, the way the grain of the wood had been matched on top, and how each piece had been fit together. And I'd thought that some day I'd like to make something like this, build a simple piece of furniture out of the best wood in the best possible way.

A few days later, I broke down and called Julie again.

"George?" her mother said. Then the pause that killed. The pause that said, I don't know if she's going to talk to you, George. The pause that said, I feel sorry for you because you're still coming around and making a fool of yourself. "I think she might be busy, George."

"Fine. It's not that important," I said.

But a second later Julie came on. "George?"

It was so unexpected, I didn't know what to say. I wasn't ready for it. I was speechless.

"Is that you, George? George, are you there?" she yodeled. "*Yoo-hoo*, George."

"Hi, it's me," I said. "Just wanted to say hello."

"Hello!" She laughed. She was high, feeling good. I knew if I asked her why, I'd only feel bad. Don't ask her, I told myself, and I asked her. "Why are you feeling so good?"

"Oooohhh, I don't know, it's a beautiful day, isn't that reason enough? How about you?"

"Yup, feeling good. Having lots of fun."

"What have you been doing?"

"This and that. Working. I have a new job."

"Ahh."

127

She didn't ask what the job was, and I couldn't stop thinking how dull I sounded. "Your cousin still around?"

"Oh, you're getting sarcastic. We better hang up."

And that was my big phone call with Julie.

One night, I lay in bed and thought about Julie, how strange it was that we were so near to each other, less than half a mile between us, she in her house and me in mine, and we didn't see each other. Never saw each other. It was as if, suddenly, we were living in two different countries with no way to cross the borders. I had no passport to her country and she didn't want one to mine. Did she ever think about me? Had it been easy for her to put me out of her mind? It still hurt when I thought about her, but more and more there were long periods when I was able to forget her completely.

Chapter 17

At Lydia's, I worked harder than I ever had for my father. I stripped and scraped and sanded and scraped and stripped and rubbed and polished. I was stripping an oak flour safe and I started going in after school to work on it. Lydia said it was an unusual piece. "Most of the cabinets people used to keep in their kitchens were pine." She loaned me a book on antiques. "Keep it as long as you want. See this?" She pointed to a picture of a lamp. "It's a Handel. Once I found a Handel at a house sale for twenty dollars."

"Is that good?" I said.

The way she laughed, I knew it wasn't too bright a question. "Is Tiffany good?" she said.

I didn't know much about Tiffany, either.

One day, she watched me working on the oak flour safe. I was wet sanding and checking for roughness and sanding again. "You have good hands, George," she said. From Lydia that was a big compliment. I mentioned it later that day to my father.

"So?" he said. "How long is this going to go on?"

"Maybe for the rest of my life."

"Very nice," my father said. "You know what you're going to do for the rest of your life after you've done it for a few weeks. Too bad the rest of the world isn't so smart."

"Don't harass me, Pop. I just know. This is what it is. I like antiques, old stuff. Is it any worse than taking someone's ratty hair and shampooing it and setting it and combing it out and making it look great? Don't you get a kick out of that?"

"That's different, that's a person. You're making a difference to a person. You make that person feel good. Her whole personality cheers up when she gets her hair fixed. Does a chair cheer up because you sand it? I like antiques, too. Does that mean I should spend the rest of my life working on old chamber pots?"

"Pop! Chamber pots!"

"I'M GOING TO SEND YOU MY PICTURE, GEORGIE. AND YOU CAN SEND ME YOURS."

"I TAKE TERRIBLE PICTURES."

"I WANT TO SEE WHAT MY FRIEND LOOKS LIKE. MAYBE WE SHOULD JUST MEET AND FORGET THE PICTURES."

"WHAT DO YOU MEAN, MEET?"

"MEET, AS IN GET ACQUAINTED, SEE EACH OTHER, ETC. YOU'RE NOT THAT FAR AWAY. DON'T YOU WANT TO MEET ME?"

I had trapped myself. "PICTURES FIRST, ROSEMARY."

But that was a trap, too, for as Rosemary reminded

me, photos had to be sent by mail and names and addresses had to be exchanged. She was Rosemary Swift, and she lived in the middle of Manhattan Island over on the East Side, on Sixty-second Street, and she had a phone number and suddenly she was somebody tangible and close. Manhattan was just across the bridge.

"WHAT'S YOUR PHONE NUMBER?" Rosemary asked.

My phone number? Of course that was next. I still didn't know how I was going to get out of the photo thing. And talk on the phone? With my voice? Just tell her the truth, I told myself, and end the deception, but instead, I gave her Lydia's shop number. Which was not too bright, but I was more worried about my parents finding out than my boss.

What a mess. Was I really going to send Rosemary my picture? That would be the end. So don't send the picture. Say it was lost in the mail. Say you have a disfiguring disease. . . . Say I'm sorry, Rosemary, I'm allergic to film. . . . I get terrible headaches when my picture is taken. . . . What I ended up doing was procrastinating.

"DID YOU SEND THE PICTURE, GEORGIE? I SENT MINE ALREADY."

"I'M GOING ON FRIDAY TO HAVE MY PICTURE TAKEN."

Friday, I "forgot," and then her picture came, but I didn't know what to do. She looked interesting. She looked better than interesting. She sent a large glossy photo that came in a brown envelope, showing her in a tuxedo and top hat. A posed studio shot. Beautiful!

I don't know what I'd expected. All time I had talked to her there were these little doubts in my mind. She said she was this and that, but you could say anything you wanted on a computer. She might have been grotesque. She might have been pimply. She might have been every ugly fantasy I could imagine. But she was none of that.

I saw that photo and I wanted more. I wanted to meet Rosemary. And how was I going to do that? She was waiting for my photo. No, she was waiting for "Georgie's" photo. Which I couldn't send. Any way I looked at it I was going to lose. And I didn't want to lose. So I pushed my luck a little bit further.

I went downtown after school, to the license bureau in the basement of City Hall. People were in line. The photo booth was off by itself in a little alcove. Nearby, a couple of girls in jeans and long shirts were filling out forms.

I went in the booth and pulled the curtain, then held it tight with my knee. I pinned on a pair of my mother's dangly earrings. I had lipstick and eyeshadow in my pocket that I'd also taken off my mother's bureau. I checked the curtain again, and smeared on lipstick. I pushed my hair in my eyes, glanced into the camera and pushed the button. *Snap.*

When the film strip came out, I looked so ridiculous, I tore it up, then pulled off the earrings and wiped off the lipstick with the back of my hand.

When I got home, I did what I should have done first. I found a snapshot of Julie and me. I was going to have to come clean sometime, but I didn't see any other way out now. In the photo, Julie was smiling directly into the camera. I was behind her, looking off over her head. On the back I wrote, "Me and Walsh." I put it in an envelope and sent it off to Rosemary.

Chapter 18

Julie!

Why aren't I talking to you anymore? Why aren't you talking to me? I'm talking to someone else and you're talking to someone else. And it's still strange and awful, because for so long we only talked to each other.

There's a place inside me for you, a place where you'll always be, a secret room that I've never shared with anybody. Julie's place. But, Julie, there's another room in my heart and it's growing and it's widening and opening up. . . . Do you care? Does it matter to you? If you knew, would you be happy, feel free of me at last? Or would you be jealous?

Rosemary and I talk at night after my sister is asleep. She thinks I'm a girl, Julie. Which is a strange thing to say, maybe a strange thing, altogether, but it doesn't feel strange when Rosemary and I are talking. What would you

133

make of that, Julie? Your George talking to another girl, girl-to-girl?

I don't know much about her, but I will soon, a whole lot more, because I want to know about her. It worries me, though, Julie. Maybe I'm scared, too. If Rosemary steps into that room, where will we be then, you and I?

In the Walshes' apartment, the lights went out. I was standing on Cliff Street with all the little houses jammed together, and I was looking across the river at the city, which looked like a mountain of light. Ten thousand thousand lights, and every light a room, and in every room someone breathing.

It was late, chilly, no one out on the street. The houses were all dark. Was Julie asleep? Maybe I'd climb the fire escape and scratch at her window.

I became aware of a car parked in front of the house. There was somebody inside the car, two somebodies. Julie. And somebody I didn't know and couldn't see, but I didn't have to see him to know it was a man.

I crossed the street. Julie looked out the window at me. Her face in the window . . . the look of her. It was Julie but different, changed, older. She was looking at me and I was looking at her.

I reached to open the door. Julie pushed the lock button down and we looked at each other through the glass like two fish in separate aquariums.

Who are you? her look said. What are you doing? It was a cautious, careful look, the way a small fish might look at a big strange fish. If we were fish, we were two fish that didn't swim in the same waters anymore.

I swung away with a sweep of my arm, as if I were holding a broad-brimmed hat with a bright feather. I

134

half bowed and let my hand sweep across the ground.
And I walked away.

Her face in the window. Her face in my head.

Julie . . .

I thought about that room in my mind, Julie's room,
and I shut the door.

Chapter 19

"There was a message for you on the answering machine," Lydia said, when I came in to work Saturday morning. "I really don't want you to have personal calls coming in on this phone."

"Sorry." Lydia was tough. Every once in a while, when I'd really worked hard on something and done it to her satisfaction, she'd crack a smile and I'd think, aha! Finally won her over. Then she'd find something to correct, helpful criticism, all low-key and matter-of-fact, but still criticism. It always made me feel like I was still tripping over my own shoelaces.

I listened to the message. "Georgie, this is Rosemary. Call me as soon as you can. 'Bye!"

I thought about it all morning, and at lunch I went out and called from an outside phone. A man answered. "Can I speak to Rosemary?" I said. I had my hand over the phone. I was feeling a little foolish, like I was in a spy movie. *Rosemary, this is Georgie. Are you wondering why I sound this way? It's not laryngitis, and I don't have a three-pack-a-day habit. The fact is I'm George, not Georgie.*

"Can you speak up?" the man said.

"Rosemary," I repeated.

"She's not here."

"Do you know when she'll be back?"

"Who is this?" It must have been her father.

"Tell her Georgie. . . . Tell her I'll call her later."

"Does this have something to do with an audition?"

"No. I'm a friend." I felt like a fool. Her father was going to know I was a guy.

All afternoon I jumped every time the phone rang. *Can I speak to Georgie?* Rosemary would say. And what would Lydia say? Wait a minute, I'll get him. *Him. Him. Him!*

As soon as I got through work, I called from the same outside phone. I was really nervous as I dialed. Be honest, I told myself. This is what you're going to say: *Rosemary, this is George. I have something I've been meaning to tell you for a long time now.*

"Hello?"

"Rosemary?"

"Georgie?"

It was her on the phone. Her voice. I'd imagined it stronger, louder, more vigorous. Her voice was almost languid and she was whispering. "Rosemary!" I was so excited to be talking to her that I forgot everything. "This is George."

"I can hardly hear you."

"You, too. It must be a bad connection."

"My father's sleeping right on the couch here. I can't

137

believe I'm finally talking to you! Listen, he's a very light sleeper. What's your number? I'll call you back from an outside phone."

I gave her my number. "I'll wait right here."

"Call you in five minutes."

I waited and thought about what I was going to say to her.

The phone rang. "Georgie? Isn't it wonderful to be really talking? Your voice is so deep. I'd love to have a voice like that."

"I like your voice."

"Georgie, your picture came yesterday. It's great! You look exactly the way I thought you would."

"I got your picture. I like the way you look. You're really a dancer, aren't you?"

"Of course I am! Didn't you believe me? We have to get together, that's all there is to it. That's what I called you about. What's a good time for you?"

"Rosemary, I want to tell you — "

"How about today? Where should we meet?"

"Today? You mean now?"

"Do you want to meet near the George Washington Bridge? I could be up at the One hundred seventy-eighth Street station in about an hour."

"I just finished work."

"Oh! You're tired. How about tomorrow?"

"I can't . . . my family."

"Monday, then, right after school?"

I ran out of excuses. "Okay," I said. It was Rosemary's idea that we both wear red berets and meet at the Port Authority downtown at four o'clock.

Monday I left school at noon. Was I really going through with this meeting? Did I dare walk up to her and say, Hi, Rosemary, I'm Georgie? Do it fast and clean, like an amputation. But was it too brutal? What if she walked away? What if I never saw her again? I began to think maybe I could dress up a little bit, disguise myself as a girl, just till she got used to me. It was a stupid idea, but I was thinking it.

I went home and took a silk blouse from my mother's closet and tucked it into my pants. I put on one of my mother's necklaces and the same pair of earrings I'd worn to the photo booth. I cinched a belt around my waist and looked at myself in the mirror. "It's not going to work," I said.

As I stood there uncertainly, the bell rang. I saw the Express Mail truck parked by the curb. The mailman rang again, and I ran down the stairs, pulling off the belt.

"Express Mail for Farina." The mailman glanced at me, then held the clipboard out for me to sign. It was a letter for my father, from Packwood & Patchen Environmental Surveys, Inc. The mailman tore off the outside receipt and handed it to me. "Nice earrings," he said.

My hand went to my ear. I'd forgotten the earrings. Heat rose to my face and I shut the door fast. I dropped the letter on the hall table and saw myself in the mirror, saw what the mailman had seen — the earrings, the tucked-in blouse. Boy pretending to be girl.

Chapter 20

I moved toward the back of the bus. I had the beret in my pocket. I glanced at the woman next to me. Her hands were folded over a rosary, and I thought of asking her to pray for me.

I was at the Port Authority before Rosemary. Or at least I thought I was. I looked around, but I didn't see a girl wearing a red beret, looking for another girl wearing a red beret.

I kept feeling the beret in my pocket. I wasn't going to put it on until I saw Rosemary and satisfied myself about her. I didn't know exactly what it was that I wanted to see, but I did know that as long as the beret was in my pocket and not on my head, I could still get out of this. I could still escape.

Swarms of people rushed through the terminal. It made me dizzy watching them. I sat down and ordered a cup of coffee. Outside on the street, yellow cabs were lined up. A black man in a white gown and a white cap was handing out religious literature. A woman in a plaid jacket was selling hot chestnuts. Near the doors, a few street people with their gear in plastic bags were dozing on the floor.

After the coffee, I bought myself a large orange juice at a stand. I was dry as a bone. Nervousness. People were coming and going in the terminal, sitting near me and behind me, eating and watching. Was one of them Rosemary, waiting to see what Georgie looked like before she raised the red beret? Waiting to see if Georgie looked like someone she wanted to know in the flesh?

For all her openness, Rosemary might have developed a pair of ice-cold feet by today and decided that getting to know me, a total stranger, was just not a smart idea.

I bought a soda and drank it too fast, but in another minute I was dry again. A pair of policemen passed, their black belts bulging with hardware, their eyes flicking over the crowd. One of them was talking into a walkie-talkie. Was I home, watching this on TV? Tonight's episode: "Stakeout at the West Side Terminal!" *George Farina, as the shortest, best-looking man on the staff, we've got a special assignment for you. Find the girl with the red beret.*

I glanced down at my hands. I usually wore my class ring on my middle finger. I pulled it off and on. My fingers were swollen. As I did it, the hair on the back of my neck rose, and I knew someone was watching me.

I swiveled around. A girl standing nearby was looking at me hard. Really looking. She was tall, that was

141

the first thing I noticed about her, and she was wearing a long man's overcoat, which made her look taller. She had a long neck and pale skin and eyes so black they seemed to have been dipped in tar. The picture didn't really say it. There was something exciting, and a little scary, about her. She looked like *somebody*. And it was her, Rosemary. I knew it even before I saw the red beret she was wearing tipped over one ear.

I produced my beret, held it up, and looked at her helplessly.

Chapter 21

"Where's Georgie?" Rosemary — because of course it was Rosemary — came toward me with an open, almost ferociously welcoming smile.

I stuffed the beret in my pocket. It was hard for me to get my eyes in focus. I was thirsty and felt a desperate need for a bathroom. All that drinking I'd been doing. "Georgie?" I started laughing, because it was a crazy, terrifying moment.

Even had I wanted to escape, there was no way I could do it anymore. Rosemary sat down next to me and put her hand over mine. "Hello! You're Walsh, aren't you?"

Walsh? For a moment I didn't get it.

"The moment I saw you, I recognized you from the picture Georgie sent me," she said. "Oh, I'm so glad to meet you! You two must have made up."

"Uh, yes, in a manner of speaking." I kept looking at her and looking away. "You could say we're in the process of getting together." I stared at her. Rosemary. This was Rosemary.

"Georgie's with you, isn't she?" she said.

"No. I mean yes, she's here, but she's not here — "

Rosemary leaned close to me. "I have to tell you, Walsh, I'm nervous about this meeting. I want Georgie to like me. I hardly slept last night."

"You, too?" I said.

"What kind of person is she? Is she very critical?"

"I don't think so. No. Georgie is — she's going to like you." I looked at her. "She does like you. I know she likes you."

She slid the salt and pepper shakers around. She had a fast, nervous way of moving and talking. "On the way here, I walked uptown from Union Square and I counted twenty red berets. I was sure everyone in the Port Authority would be wearing red berets. But the funny thing is, I wasn't even looking for a beret when I walked in. I knew I'd recognize Georgie. Then I saw you, instead, and I recognized you. I thought, That's Walsh. He and Georgie must have made up." She put her hand over her mouth. "I'm talking too much."

"You know, Rosemary, Georgie's not going to be just what you expect."

"Oh, I know she's not ordinary."

"You know how you get a certain idea about somebody, and no matter what the real thing about them is, it's hard to shake your original idea."

"What does that mean?" she said. She kept looking around. "You're making me nervous, Walsh." She ordered a glass of milk. Our eyes met and she smiled at

144

me and patted me on the shoulder. It was more than a pat; she left her hand on my shoulder. "It's nice that you and Georgie made up."

Her hand on my shoulder and those warm looks . . . those looks were going right through me.

She took a sip of the milk, made a face, and pushed it away. "I hate milk."

"Why'd you order it?"

"My father says it's good for me. Don't you always do what your father tells you to?" And she gave me a wide-eyed look, and then she laughed.

Her eyes, those dark, tarry eyes! Rosemary. She'd been a name, words on a screen, a whispery voice on the phone. Rosemary. She was beyond anything I'd ever expected. It was wonderful to be here with her. And I could tell — I was pretty sure — she liked me, too.

"Where did you say Georgie was? What's taking her so long?"

"She's here," I said.

Rosemary stood up and looked around. "I don't see her."

"Here," I said, pointing to myself. "Right here. Rosemary, sit down. I want to tell you something." It was a relief to say it. "Rosemary — I'm not Walsh."

"What do you mean you're not Walsh?"

"I'm George Farina."

"Who?"

"George Farina."

"Wait a minute. Wait a minute! Your name is Walsh."

"No. Farina."

"That's Georgie's name."

"That's right. That's my name."

"You're her brother? That picture was of you and

her?" She clapped her head to her head. "Oh, oh, oh! I get it. Georgie doesn't really have a boyfriend, and she didn't want me to know. Oh, I don't care about stuff like that! Poor Georgie! What is she doing? Is she here? Is she hiding, waiting for you to call her?"

"Rosemary," I said. "Rosemary. Listen. There is no Georgie. There's just me. George Farina."

"Wait a second. Now stop. Stop." She put her hands over her ears. "Let me think about this. I come here expecting to meet my friend Georgie. Instead, you're here. And I know you, I recognized you from the picture. Now you're telling me you're not Walsh; you're George Farina. Fine. But where's Georgie?"

"No Georgie," I said.

"There is no Georgie?"

"No."

"Okay, if she's not here, tell me where she is."

"She isn't anywhere. She doesn't exist."

"I don't get it." She sat back in her seat. "I just don't get it. Of course there's a Georgie. I talked to her yesterday."

"No, you talked to me. George Farina. I'm George and I'm Georgie."

There was a long silence. Then she said, "Is this some kind of a game? Am I being set up? Is there a hidden camera here? Do you have a microphone somewhere?" She reached across the counter and picked up my collar. "I'm not very good at games."

"It's not a game. I'm trying to explain — "

She fished around in her pocket. I half expected her to come out with a gun and blow me away, but it was the photo I'd sent her of me and Julie. "That's you."

"Yes. Me. George Farina."

"Not Walsh?"

146

"That's Walsh." I pointed to Julie. "My old girl-friend. Julie Walsh."

Rosemary turned the photo over and read the words. "Me and Walsh."

"I didn't lie," I said. "It is me and Walsh."

Rosemary stood up and I stood, too, conscious in a way I hadn't been before that she was taller than me. "You're telling me that all this time I thought I was talking to Georgie on the computer, to a girl, it was you?"

"Yes."

"You made believe you were a girl?"

"Rosemary, I didn't set out to do it, it just happened."

"You said you worked in a beauty parlor."

"I do. I work for my father. Men work in beauty parlors."

"You didn't correct me, you let me believe you were a girl. You knew that's what I thought! You never said you were a boy."

"I was going to, but I was afraid you'd stop talking to me."

"You did that on purpose. You tricked me." And then she got really hostile. "Who are you? What are you doing here? What do you want? Why did you come?"

"You said you wanted to meet me."

"Not you! I never said I wanted to meet *you*. I don't want you! I want Georgie."

"I am Georgie, Rosemary."

"No! You're not! No way are you Georgie. She's my friend. What are you? I don't even know you. *Who are you?*"

"George," I said again, watching her. There was a

147

glitter, a shine, a coldness in her eyes that scared me. "Rosemary, don't think what you're thinking. I was going to tell you the truth."

"The truth? You liar! You don't know what the truth is." She slapped me.

"Hey! That hurt." But it wasn't that. I felt embarrassed in front of everyone.

"Hurt?" she said. "I'm the one who's hurt. Are you bizarre or what?" And then she slapped me again, hit me in the face.

I was still trying to be reasonable. "Look, what difference does it make? It's just a name. You want to call me Georgie, that's okay. Call me anything you want. Can't we be friends, at least?"

"Go to hell," she said, and she walked away. Oh, she walked, she stalked, she marched away.

I didn't know what to do. She had acted like I was something disgusting, something stinking and rotten. She'd hit me. She hated me. I watched her go, disappear into the crowd. I was never going to see her again. Then I went after her.

I caught a glimpse of her on the corner. She was easy to spot. She was tall, had broad shoulders, and she was moving fast. When the light changed, she was across before I even got to the corner. Then I got caught in the middle of traffic. Buses, cars, taxis were all trying to destroy me. "Rosemary," I yelled. She was walking toward Broadway past the movie arcades, the triple X-rated sex flicks, and the touristy junk places.

I caught her halfway down the block. I tapped her on the shoulder. "Here I am — "

She swung at me, but I was ready this time and blocked her punch with my arm. But I forgot about her other hand. She punched me in the stomach. A man walking by laughed.

I caught up to her again on the corner near the subway entrance. When she saw me, she raised her fist.

"I only want to talk — " I began.

"Don't come near me. You terrible person. Getting me to trust you. '*I'm your girlfriend.*' " There were tears in her eyes. "It's not *easy* for me to make friends," she said in a strained voice. "And I believed you. I really thought I had a friend."

"I am your friend!"

She sped down a flight of stairs to the subway and I followed, fishing around in my pocket for a token. I had to stand in line at the change booth. Rosemary disappeared into the crowd. I heard a train, panicked, and jumped over the turnstile, then saw it was on the other side, on the other platform, and I jumped back. The woman in the change booth was yelling at me. "Sorry, sorry," I said, and I pushed the money at her. A man was playing a violin in the middle of the platform. It was familiar music, classical, something I'd heard Troy play more than once. I found Rosemary there near the violinist. When he finished, she dropped some coins into his open case.

I threw in a dollar, and she turned and saw me. "Oh," she said. "You."

"Was he playing Bach?" I said. "Or was it Handel? I can never tell the difference."

She just looked at me. "You know what?" she said suddenly. "I gave you a black eye."

The minute she said it, my left eye started aching. I held my hand to my face. "You really bashed me."

"I should have killed you."

She wasn't exactly calmed down, but she wasn't swinging. "Can we talk now?" I asked.

"Does that eye hurt?"

"It throbs a little."

"I didn't mean to do *that*."

"No, you just wanted to kill me."

"Yes, but cleanly." She looked at me calmly. "I should be sorry, but I'm not. Beating you up made me feel much better."

"Anytime you want a punching bag," I said. I thought the worst was over. "I know I'm going to take a little getting used to, but if Georgie is your friend, so is George. I'm just like her, even if I did make a lousy girl."

"You made a *terrific* girl, you creep."

A train came into the station. She glanced around as people came off.

"Can't we sit down somewhere?" I said. "There's a lot I want to explain to you." I was planning to start at the beginning, with Julie and how miserable I'd been, and work up from there. "There's a bench over there."

"Lead the way," she said.

I thought she was behind me, but when I looked back, she was on the train, and the doors were shutting. I ran to get in, but she pushed me. She'd timed it perfectly. I was outside and she was inside.

I ran alongside the train, tapping on the window as it started to move. "That was tricky, Rosemary," I yelled. "My hat's off to you." I waved the beret at her as the train picked up speed. But as it disappeared, I thought, There goes Rosemary, and I got really depressed.

150

Chapter 22

"ROSEMARY, COME BACK TO 'GO.' REMEMBER MONOPOLY, ROSEMARY? YOU MUST HAVE PLAYED IT. WHEN YOU CROSS 'GO,' YOU COLLECT $100 AND START AGAIN. THAT'S WHAT I WANT TO DO, START THE GAME ALL OVER AGAIN. YOUR MARKER IS A TOP HAT. MINE'S A BEAUTY PARLOR. YOU ROLL FIRST.

"REMEMBER, THAT'S THE WAY WE MET, BY ACCIDENT, A ROLL OF THE DICE. MOVE SIX SPACES OR TWELVE. I LANDED ON YOUR PROPERTY AND WE HAD A GOOD TIME TALKING. SO WHAT WENT WRONG? THERE WERE STEPS. ALL MISTAKES HAPPEN STEP BY STEP. ALL GOOD THINGS HAPPEN STEP BY STEP, AND ALL BAD THINGS HAPPEN THE SAME WAY. I DIDN'T SET OUT TO DO SOMETHING BAD. I JUST NEEDED SOMEONE TO TALK TO.

"IN THE BEGINNING THERE WAS BEAUTY PARLOR AND TOP HAT. THERE WAS YOU AND ME. THERE WERE TWO

151

PEOPLE. TWO VOICES. AND WE TALKED AND BECAME
FRIENDS. AND YOU BECAME ROSEMARY AND I BECAME
GEORGIE.

"YOU WANTED A GIRLFRIEND. I WANTED SOMEONE TO
TALK TO. SO TOGETHER WE MADE GEORGIE. WHEN I
FOUND OUT YOU WERE A GIRL AND YOU THOUGHT I
WAS, TOO, IT BECAME PART OF THE GAME — HOW LONG
COULD I KEEP YOU FROM KNOWING WITHOUT LYING?
YOU SAID YOU DON'T LIKE GAMES, BUT I DO. I COULDN'T
STOP PLAYING. I SHOULD HAVE. WHEN I STOPPED AT
COMMUNITY CHEST, I SHOULD HAVE PULLED OUT A CARD
THAT SAID, 'COLLECT $75 AND TURN INTO GEORGE.'
INSTEAD, I DREW A CARD THAT SAID, 'GO TO JAIL.'

"MAYBE WE SHOULD STOP PLAYING GAMES. LET'S GET
REAL, ROSEMARY. WE MET. YOU SAW ME AND I SAW YOU.
YOU'RE ROSEMARY AND I'M GEORGE. I MIGHT BE WRONG,
BUT I THINK YOU LIKE ME. I KNOW I LIKE YOU. ISN'T
THAT ENOUGH TO START? I WANT TO BE FRIENDS. DO
YOU?"

Chapter 23

In the next few days, I kept checking the computer bulletin board. Every time the phone rang, I thought of Rosemary. We had to talk. Let her say whatever she was going to say, get it out of her system. I had to call her. But the call was so important, I couldn't pick up the phone. Was this the right time? Should I call later? Midnight? First thing in the morning? And what should my first words be? Hello? Brilliant.

I finally called at seven one evening. Not too early. Not too late. I didn't expect success; I expected her father. Or an answering machine, or nothing. Rosemary answered on the first ring. "Hello, hello!" Like she'd been sitting there, waiting for someone to call.

"This is George," I said.

"Oh. I can't talk to you — "

"Rosemary, listen. Give me one minute at least."

"I'm on my way out to an audition."

"Where? I'll meet you there."

Silence.

"I'm not a pervert."

Silence.

"All I want to do is talk, Rosemary. I promise I'll go away the minute you tell me to."

"I can't talk at an audition. I have to concentrate on what I'm doing."

"Understood. I promise, not a word till after it's over."

"I'll probably be there till midnight."

"That's okay. I don't turn into a pumpkin. Where is it?"

"God, you're persistent!"

"I have other good qualities, too."

She finally gave me an address off Amsterdam Avenue.

It was nine o'clock when I got there. The church was an old building with wide stone steps that led to a pair of massive doors that opened with surprising ease. Inside, in the entry, there was a penciled notice: AUDITION DOWNSTAIRS. I followed the arrow.

I heard music as I went down. It was a big basement room, columns and open space with a piano and people sitting around on folding chairs. The dancers were everywhere, sitting and standing, in their leotards and leg warmers. I saw Rosemary in a purple leotard with her long coat over her shoulders. She didn't notice me coming in.

I sat down. The director was a tall, balding man in a Hawaiian shirt. There was a woman next to him, writing in a notebook. I heard someone call him Davis. "Moscowitz," he called. A short chunky boy bounced up. "Give me a little modern jazz," he said to the pianist. The dancer was amazing. He was like a rubber ball, bouncing off the floor. After he did a few routines, the director tried him on country music, then African. "Okay," he said finally. "Next."

Myers was next, then Ogilvie. Rosemary was still waiting. The way she was sitting, holding her coat around her, I felt the tension she was under. The director was abrupt, quick; his decisions came snap, snap, snap. One dancer hardly began and he said, "Thank you. Next." No praise, no encouragement. One dancer after another. He let one dancer go on and on, and the whole time he was turned around, talking to a man and woman behind him.

When Rosemary's turn came, I leaned forward, a little sweaty and tense for her. Was she good? Would she be good enough? She came out quickly, letting her coat fall dramatically to the floor. A man I hadn't noticed before picked it up. An older man. Was that her father?

Rosemary stood, long, perfect legs in a purple leotard, her hands folded in front of her. Then, as the music began, she started dancing. She was good. I thought she was better than the other dancers, but maybe I was prejudiced. Her dancing was smooth and seemed to flow from one movement to another. She never looked clumsy. Davis didn't cut her off, he didn't say anything to her, either. And I didn't see him whispering to his assistant to write anything in her notebook.

I went up to Rosemary as soon as she finished. "You were great," I said.

She made a nervous, negative gesture. Her hands were clenched. I felt the heat come off her. She sat

155

down again with the other dancers. Nobody left till the last dancer had tried out.

The director conferred with the woman with the notebook and the couple behind him. Then he stood by the piano and told a few of the dancers to stay. "Allen, Kerenski, Moscowitz. . . ." He thanked everyone else. "We have your phone numbers. We know where to reach you."

That was it. Everyone got up to leave. It was almost eleven o'clock. I waited by the stairs for Rosemary. "I was awful," she said.

"You were good," I said.

"Don't talk about it! I was awful. You don't know anything about it."

"I'm no expert, but I know what I saw. You were one of the best."

"One of the best isn't good enough. This is New York! Do you know how many talented dancers there are around?"

The older man I'd noticed before joined us outside. "So, you see, I got here," he said to Rosemary.

"I know."

"Are you glad I came?"

She shrugged, but when she turned to me, she made a face.

"Davis is a beast," the man said. "He acts like this is Broadway, Rosie."

"They're all like that." She started walking rapidly down the street, with me and this guy behind her. Snow was slowly falling and melting as it hit the street.

"Rosie's wonderful," the man said to me. "Look at the way she moves. Look at her back. She's very special. She's going to be successful because she is so special."

The snow was settling in Rosemary's hair and on her shoulders. I had an idea she didn't like this guy, but the way he said her name — *Rosie . . .* dragging it out — he seemed to know her really well.

"I'm Jasper," he said to me, as if that said it all. "I'm a sculptor, I have an interest in all the arts, especially dancing. They inspire my work. Rosie is very talented." He raised his voice on the last line.

Rosemary shrugged.

He pulled a wallet full of pictures out of his pocket and started showing me the things he made. He was a big man with big hands, but everything he made was tiny. He said they were dance sculptures, but they didn't look like anything to me but little stick figures.

Jasper took a cigarette and stuck it in the corner of his mouth. "Rosie, do you have a match?"

She handed him a lighter over her shoulder.

"You smoke?" I said to Rosemary.

She shook her head. "I wouldn't. I'm a dancer. But I always carry a lighter."

I took a cigarette from him. "Bad habit," he said and lit it for me. "What's your name?"

"That's Georgie," Rosemary called back.

It sounded sarcastic as hell. Did she even want me here? I'd invited myself.

"Did you read that article they did on me in the *Village Voice?*" Jasper said.

I took a puff of the cigarette and shook my head. An article in a newspaper? That was high-powered stuff. Was something going on between him and Rosemary? I couldn't compete with that.

"An article?" Rosemary said. "Isn't that piling it on? It was just a notice of a show."

"But in the *Village Voice*," Jasper said. "That carries clout."

Rosemary was hungry. We stopped to eat in a deli, a takeout place with a few tables. There were salamis hanging in the window and a big loaf of rye bread on a cutting board. It smelled great in there. Jasper ordered cheesecake and then complained that it was too sticky. He didn't like the look of Rosemary's sandwich, either. The corned beef was too fatty. The bread was stale. The pickle was soggy.

"How's your sandwich?" he asked. I'd ordered a ham and cheese.

"Perfect," I said. Rosemary gave me a little smile.

When the bill came, Jasper passed it to Rosemary. "I'm a little short. The next time, I'll get it."

I couldn't believe this guy. "Don't you have anything?" I said. "Your cheesecake was three dollars."

"They charge too much for their lousy food. I'll take care of the tip." He put a quarter on the table and went outside.

Rosemary and I split the bill. "Take your time," she said. "Want a stick of gum?" She unwrapped it slowly. "Maybe Jasper'll go away."

"Isn't he a friend of yours?"

"He's a pest, is what he is. I can't get rid of him. Every time I show up for an audition, he's there."

Outside, Jasper was waiting, chewing on a toothpick. He handed me one. "It's free, Georgie." He put his arm across Rosemary's shoulders. "The night's young. What do we do now?"

She slipped out from under his arm. "I better get home," she said.

158

He got his arm around her again. "How about you, Jersey?" he said to me. "Don't the buses stop running out to the boonies after midnight?"

Rosemary gave me a look over Jasper's head that said, Don't go away. Don't leave me with him.

Right at that moment, something changed between us.

We walked around for another hour, eating ice-cream cones and listening to Jasper's line of bull. His work, his art, his delicacy. . . . On and on and on. It was nearly one o'clock. The guy was never going to shut up. Rosemary couldn't stop yawning.

"Are you listening, Rosie?" Jasper said.

"To what?" She yawned.

I slumped against a building. "We're both listening." I yawned a couple of times, too, and Rosemary started giggling. Then I started giggling, and we couldn't stop.

Jasper looked from one to the other of us. "I'll see you around, Rosie," he said, and he walked away.

"We teed him off," Rosemary said. "Were we awful? Was that really mean?"

"He deserved it," I said.

Chapter 24

"Mom?" I said. "Did I wake you up?"

"George? George, where are you? I've been worried sick! Do you know what time it is? Did something happen? Are you okay?"

"Mom, give me a chance to explain. I'm at a friend's house."

"What kind of explanation is that? It's the middle of the night. It's two o'clock in the morning, George! I want to know — "

"I'm in the city and — "

"New York? What are you doing there?"

"I can explain the whole thing to you. I have a friend in New York and I came over to see her audition — "

"Since when do you have a friend in New York?"

"It's the first time we ever heard anything about her," my father said.

"Oh, you're on the line, too, Dad? Great. A family conference. Why don't you guys go back to bed? I'm okay, I just wanted to let you know, I'll see you in the morning."

"You're staying with a girl overnight?" my father said. "Who else is there?"

"No one, right now."

"Where are her parents?"

"Her father's out. He should be back any moment."

"Where's her mother?"

"Dad, do we have to go into this now? Why do you have to know?"

"George, we're the parents. We ask the questions."

"The answer is, they're divorced. I'll be home tomorrow; you can put me on the stand again." And I hung up.

"They really quizzed you, didn't they?" Rosemary said. "That was your mother and your father both?"

"They don't stop me from doing what I want," I said defensively.

"I think it's great having both your parents on your case."

That surprised me. "I thought you couldn't stand your parents."

"I like my mother and father. It's my stepfather I can't bear. Well . . . my mother bugs me a little, too. I want her to stand up to my stepfather and she doesn't. I like parents who keep tabs on their kids, maybe because I never had it. My father was always disappearing when I was a little kid, and my mother's wishy-washy."

"I thought you thought your father was so great."

161

"He's a great person. That doesn't make him a great father. A great father is there for his kids. Right? Your father sounds like a great father."

"He is." We were looking at each other across the couch, and I thought about kissing her. What were we talking about our parents for? "Rosemary. . . . " I leaned toward her.

"Let me see, you're going to need clean sheets," she said, and she went to get them.

I followed her. "Rosemary. . . . " She took sheets and a blanket out of a closet. It was a narrow space and I was standing in her way. I was close. "Rosemary . . . " I said again.

"Please. A little space."

I followed her back into the living room and we made up the couch together. "I never thought this was the way things would end tonight," I said.

"What do you mean?"

"I mean, here I am. In your house. Going to sleep on your couch. Where were we this morning?"

"Nowhere."

"That's the point. I just called you this evening. You didn't even want to talk to me."

"I talked to you."

"Don't forget, the last time I saw you, you punched me in the eye."

She tucked a sheet under the couch pillows and pulled it tight. "Don't get any ideas. You helped me out tonight — I wasn't going to let you sleep in the bus station."

"Is that the only reason?"

"Look, it's late and I'm tired. It's obviously not the only reason. I don't let just anybody come in the house. My father's going to be home soon. And no matter

162

what you think, I'm still not used to you. I haven't forgotten Georgie."

"Okay, understood."

"And I don't make friends easily."

"Understood."

"But if I do, it's a friend for life."

"Well, that makes me hopeful."

"Right," she said and went off to the bathroom.

So where did I stand with her? I'd seen two Rosemarys, or maybe three or four, this evening. There was that pleading Rosemary (*Don't leave me alone with him!*), and Queen Rosemary with her crown of snowflakes, marching down the street with her attendants running behind her, and now this Rosemary, cautious and reserved and sincere and protecting herself. And I liked all of them.

I was half asleep when I heard her father come in. I kept my eyes closed. I felt him standing near me. I smelled cigarettes and the outdoors. He went past and I heard a door open, then a moment later, Rosemary's voice.

I drifted off to sleep again. The next time I woke up, it was nearly morning. There was a pale light in the room. I got off the couch and got dressed. Then I went in the kitchen and drank a glass of water. It was six-thirty when I left the apartment.

Chapter 25

"George, wait a minute," Rosemary called, coming after me. "Where're you going?"

The elevator doors slid open. "I have to go to work."

"I'll go down with you."

We went down in the elevator together, not talking. "I don't talk a lot in the morning," she said.

"Me, either," I said.

But then, when we went out, she gave me a really nice smile, and I felt that she had come out because of me.

It was cold and gray out. I walked to the bakery with her. She bought rolls for her father's breakfast. "Do you want some coffee?" she asked.

"What are you having?"

"Cocoa."

We got two cocoas and a couple of donuts and sat

164

down at a little table against the wall. Rosemary didn't look so much like an actress this morning. She looked plainer. "You look different," I said.

"My morning face. No mascara."

I glanced at my watch.

"Do you have to go right away?" she asked.

"My boss is tough," I said. "I can't be late." And I told her how Lydia had chewed me out the first day I came to work.

"Lydia? Oh, I remember. That was the job Georgie was trying to get."

Every time she said "Georgie," I looked at her to see how she meant it. I wanted to forget Georgie, and I wanted Rosemary to forget "her," too.

That afternoon I went over to Leonard's after work. "Hello, George," the woman in my father's chair said.

"Oh, hello, Mrs. Bucci." I admired the haircut my father had given her. "Very becoming."

"Don't go away," my father said. "I want to talk to you." He lit a cigarette and drew me aside. "Well, what's the story?"

"What story?"

"Last night."

"I missed the last bus, so I slept over in New York."

"This girl is from New York City? The girls around here aren't exciting enough for you?"

"Dad, cut it out."

He gave me a going-over about Rosemary. Who was she? What was her family like? She left her home? "Why does a girl leave home at fifteen?"

"Sixteen, Dad."

"I'm just curious. First, things are off with Julie, which I still don't understand, and now, this girl in New York." More questions. Where had I met Rosemary? Through the computer? What kind of way was that to meet a person? Where did she go to school? Was her family Italian?

I finally escaped. My mother was on the phone but motioned me to wait. When she hung up, she said, "That girl you stayed with — who is she? I don't want to be nosy, I just want to get the facts straight."

"Her name's Rosemary. I stayed in her apartment. Not in her bed. On the couch. Do you catch the distinction, Mom? Her father was there the whole time."

"He wasn't there when you called me."

I leaned on the counter. Had my parents always been this way? Had I been taking it all this time and not knowing it? I used to go around bragging, saying I could say anything to my parents, they were my friends. "Rosemary's father came home, Mom. If you want to know, did I sleep alone — "

"Yes?"

"Mom! I always thought you were so cool."

"Not with all this AIDS talk. Not when it has to do with my child."

"Child, Mom? Joanne, yes. But me? You think I would do something dumb?"

"George." She took my chin. "Why did you stay at her house last night?"

"Mom, as I told you and Dad, I missed the last bus. Did you want me to sleep in the Port Authority?"

"You could have called us. We would have come over."

"Mom, I'm almost eighteen," I said, and I got out of there.

Rosemary and I talked on the phone almost every night that week. We got to know each other again. I

166

thought we'd dropped Georgie, but Rosemary didn't forget. Every once in a while, she'd remind me. "Come on, talk to me, Georgie. Are we girlfriends or not?"

Friday night she called and said, "Checking up on you, Farina. Want to come over and have breakfast Sunday morning?"

"What's it going to be?"

"Rat poison sprinkled on broken glass."

"Oh, so you do like me a little?" I said.

"You're growing on me."

"Like a fungus."

"Enough small talk, Farina. Are you coming or not?"

"No. You come here this time." I said it just like that, but when she said yes, I let out a yell.

Rosemary came over Saturday, and I quit work early so I could meet her bus. I had to promise Lydia two extra hours next week.

"Snow!" Rosemary said when she got off the bus. "Do you know how long it's been since I've seen real snow?" She had to make a snowball right away and throw it at a sign. She was wearing her long coat and jeans and the red beret. I hugged her, and she let me keep my arm around her.

This was only the third time I'd seen her, but each time was like the first time. There was something surprising about her. She was always more vivid than what I imagined. I suppose I still wasn't used to her. Maybe it was the effect of having been on the computer with her so long. There was so much color and energy and warmth in the real Rosemary.

"Well, here it is," I said. "Historic Clifton Heights." I was a little nervous. Rosemary was New York City. Men like Jasper, who talked about art, chased after her. Even if he was a jerk, it was unnerving. What

167

did Clifton Heights have to offer her? Looked at from the point of view of a smart New Yorker, it was just a place to sleep at night.

"Oh, it's really a small town," Rosemary said.

"Sickening, right?"

"I can't believe New York's just across the river. Look at those empty side streets! Look at all the dogs running around loose."

"Dog mecca of the world," I said. "Pay attention, please. We're now passing through downtown. Over there is the store where my father had his first business. Now a travel agency. Notice the village post office. And the village constabulary. And over here, we have the Sweetheart Shopping Mall, where everyone who's anyone shops."

"I love it," she said. "It's just like home."

I looked at her but she was serious.

"I never thought I'd hear myself saying that," she admitted. "I'm a real cornflake, and I don't even know it."

We walked over to my parents' place. "Do they know we're coming?" Rosemary asked. "Are we being watched? Are the neighbors telephoning ahead? If it was Champion, you can bet they would be."

The purple awnings and the flag outside Leonard's impressed Rosemary. "This is classy. This is your parents' place? They own it?"

"Just your typical little beauty parlor," I said.

We went in. "Mom," I said, "it's my pleasure to introduce you to" — Rosemary gave me a nudge — "Mom, this is my friend, Rosemary Swift." Then I brought Rosemary over to my father. He stopped work, shook hands with her, and started interrogating her.

"Do you live around here?" He knew where she

lived. "How long have you lived in New York?" He probably knew that, too.

"We've got to move along, Dad." I pulled Rosemary over to show her the photographs on the wall. "Here, we have all the famous people my father has shaken hands with. You recognize this guy?"

"Of course. The Boss."

I took her around and introduced her to everyone. Before we left, I asked my father for the car to bring Rosemary home, but he refused. He didn't want me driving into the city. "I'll be careful," I said, but it was still no.

Rosemary and I stopped for a pizza. "Now I know your parents," she said, folding her pizza. "I'm filling in the gaps. Who's next? Your sister?"

"Joanne's away on a science trip with her friend Ernie Paik and some other kids. You could meet Troy, though."

"Great! And Julie? No, no, no." She laughed, and wiped her mouth. "Forget that. I don't really want to meet her. I'd just like to *see* her. I'm curious about her."

"Okay, let's go over to her house," I said.

It was an impulse. I didn't know if it was a good idea. Did I really want the two of them to meet? Maybe I wanted Julie to see that I was all right. More than all right. Did I want to make her jealous? Did I even care? I didn't know the answer to any of those questions.

And I didn't find out, either, because Julie wasn't around. We looked out over the cliff to New York City, then we walked over to Troy's house and spoke to his mother. Troy wasn't home.

That was the day. Nothing exciting, but I was excited. Just being with Rosemary was exciting. When it was time for her to go, we were still talking. She said another audition was coming up. "I'm going to do better. I know what I have to work on."

"Here comes the bus," I said, but we let it go by.

I wanted to kiss her, but I still wasn't completely sure how we stood with each other. I knew we were friends.

"I should catch the next one," she said, and then she let that one go by, too. "The next one for sure." She was laughing. "Yes or no?"

I kept thinking about that kiss. Too many people around. Too many distractions. Across the street, a parking lot. Down the block, a Dumpster. There was a tree nearby — that looked good — but there were kids playing there. No privacy. Not very romantic. This is a hell of a place for a kiss, I thought, and I kissed her.

Chapter 26

I worked the whole winter vacation. I was saving money with the vague thought of buying myself a car. I didn't want to keep asking my parents every time I wanted wheels and either be refused or have to worry about my father inspecting the car for scratches. The cars were theirs. My mother's car. My father's car. And the place we lived — it was theirs, too. It was my parents' house.

I heard myself saying it. My *parents'* house? Where did that come from? It had always been *our* car and *our* house. My room, my refrigerator, where I lived. I remembered the night I stayed over at Rosemary's and being aware of her standing there, listening, while I explained myself to my parents. She wasn't making those kinds of explanations for every little move she made. I never resented my parents before. Maybe it was just that I was getting older — I was almost eighteen. When do you stop needing your parents' permission?

On New Year's Day, when nobody was at the store, Lydia's place was broken into. I was the first one there the next morning. There was a police car in the parking lot. The door to the shop was open and the big plate glass window in front was smashed. A policeman came out from the back. "Who are you?" he said.

"George Farina. I work here."

"Don't move." He had a flashlight in one hand and a nightstick in the other. "Let me see your ID."

He looked at my driver's license and my school cafeteria card. "When was the last time you were here?"

"Day before yesterday."

"Stand over there. Put that bike down. Drop it. Where were you last night?"

"Me? Home." Was he going to believe that? "You can check with my parents." Then I remembered I'd gone over to Troy's and we'd talked till after midnight.

"Who else was with you?"

"My sister. Then I visited my friend."

"What time?"

"Around nine o'clock."

He had me bend over the car. "Get your hands up. Over the top of the hood. Spread your legs."

Here it comes, I thought. George, your life is not dull anymore. Now you're going to get frisked. I laughed. I didn't mean to. It was a nervous laugh, but it irritated him and he put the cuffs on me.

Oh, this is great, I thought. Wait till I tell Rosemary. Then Lydia drove up in her Blazer. Her tires crunched over the broken glass. "Lydia!" I held up my cuffed hands.

172

She got out of the car. It still took a few minutes of talking before the cuffs came off. "You've got a problem with your attitude," the cop said to me.

We went inside. The break-in was vandalism. Brainless stuff. Some idiots celebrating New Year's had pushed bookcases over, smashed one of the antique glassfronts, and hacked apart a set of ladderback chairs.

"Did you lock up when you left the other night?" the cop asked Lydia.

"Of course I locked up."

"No alarm system here."

"I haven't had the money to install one. I can never understand why anyone would want to rob a place like this." She looked suddenly exhausted.

The cop toed a beer can under his foot. "Is this yours?"

"I don't drink when I work and I don't drink that cheap sludge. What are you going to do about this?"

"I'll make out a report. We'll be talking to people, see if anybody saw anything."

"What if these bums come back?"

"Usually they don't hit the same place twice."

"But what if they do?" she insisted.

"We'll do the best we can for you. You better get yourself a burglar alarm and a guard dog."

"I'm allergic to dogs."

After the cop left, Lydia was really steaming. "Did you see him writing things down? A report! That's all they're going to do, make a report. They'll never catch anyone." We made an inventory of the damage. Lydia picked up a drawer. It came from a Stickley piece. "George, see if you can find the desk." She sat down on the floor. "I feel sick."

It took us all day to clean up, put aside things that

could be repaired, and junk the rest. Later, I took the Blazer and drove to Paramus to buy half-inch plywood to board up the windows. That was tomorrow's job. Temporarily we hung sheets of plastic. Then Lydia had to go home to take care of her baby. But she was worried because the store was essentially wide open.

"If you want me to, I could stay here tonight," I said.

"Would you? I was thinking of coming back, but I don't know if I can get a baby-sitter. Dan — my husband — works nights."

"No, I'll stay."

"Thanks," she said, and the way she said it made me feel really good.

I called my mother to tell her, and I got an argument. "Why?" she said. "You don't have to do it. It's not your place, and if Lydia needs a watchman, she can hire someone."

"She's hired me."

"You're not a guard. What if they come back? It could be dangerous."

"Come on, Mom, it was just a bunch of drunken jerks."

"You don't know that, George. Don't act like it's a lark."

"Mom, I'll call you tomorrow."

"George, call me tonight before you go to sleep."

"Good-bye, Mom."

I didn't sleep a lot that night. In the back there was a windowless storeroom with a door to the outside and another door that opened to the workroom. With the inside door open, it was warm enough, and I could see into the store. I slept on a folding cot.

All night long, the plastic over the broken window

rustled. I kept waking up and flashing my light around. I had a baseball bat under the cot. Sometimes cars went speeding by, and a couple of times sirens brought me awake, and I lay there, listening.

Once I was sure someone was inside, tiptoeing around. "Hey!" I jumped up and turned on the lights, but it was nothing. I couldn't go back to sleep after that, so I pulled the phone in from the other room and dialed Rosemary. If her father answered, I'd hang up.

Rosemary answered. "George?" she said.

"How'd you know it was me?"

"Who else would call me in the middle of the night?"

We talked for a long time. Rosemary was telling me about a letter she'd gotten from her favorite brother when I fell asleep. I woke up to hear her saying, ". . . think I should go for a visit?"

"Where?"

"Aren't you listening?"

"Wherever it is, don't go. Scratch that. I'm being selfish." I must have fallen asleep again. When I woke up, I had the phone on the pillow. "Rosemary?"

"Uhhh. . . ." She'd been asleep, too.

"It's me," I said.

"Sing to me," she said.

I started singing some old corny song. *"On top of old Smokeeee. . . ."*

"Nice," she murmured and sang with me.

Julie and I never sang. I didn't even know I could sing.

I woke in the morning, the phone against my ear. "Rosemary?" Listening, I could hear her breathing. And I imagined her curled up on the couch, sleeping, with the phone against her lips.

175

Chapter 27

A few weeks later, on the way home from work I saw Julie driving by in her father's blue Pinto. It was a warmish wintery day. I'd just bought a couple of apples and a wedge of cheddar cheese. "Julie!" She had stopped for a light. I tapped on the window and got in. "How about a ride?"

She didn't say anything. I presented her with an apple that I polished on my sleeve. "You look good, Julie." She was wearing corduroys and a sweater.

I took a bite out of the apple. I offered her the cheese, and in my mind I thought, I'm doing this perfectly. I'm so together, I'm so at ease. I'm probably dazzling her. "How's your life these days? You and the significant other?"

"Significant other?"

"What they used to call boyfriend."

"I've got other things on my mind."

"School? Have you made a decision?"

"Fairleigh Dickinson."

"Wise. Not far from home. That's practical. Why spend money on room and board when you can go to school and live at home? Room and board. No pun intended." But then I explained it, because she wasn't responding to anything I said.

"Room and b-o-r-e-d," I said and got the same exciting response. "No slur intended against your family. How are your parents?" Still no response. "This is a sincere and heartfelt question, Julie. How are they? I always liked your mom and dad."

"George, shut up," she said, and she gave me a furious look.

"What?"

"What? What? You know what!"

"Maybe I ought to get out right here, Julie."

She stopped the car.

"Give me back my apple."

"Very funny, George. Did you get a laugh when you read the story in the *Clifton Courier*? Was it a thrill seeing it on TV? Is your father going to buy you a little sports car now?"

"What are you talking about?"

"I'm talking about the fabulous offer Muggleston Developers made for the property on One-thirteen Cliffside."

"My father's building?"

"Your father's former building. My family's former home. We've got six months to vacate."

"No," I said.

"Don't tell me no, George. It's sold. A million dollars."

"My father?"

"Your father, who was never going to sell our house. He loved this town so much he was never going to let the developers in, no matter how much money he was offered. Right, George? He was going to keep the town the way it was. Right? Remember the lecture he gave us once about little towns being the heart of America and how everything good was in the little town and everything bad was in the big city? That impressed me. I thought your father was so smart."

"My father's not doing that," I said. I was stunned. I didn't know why Julie was saying it. There had to be a mistake. "A million dollars?" My father hadn't said a word about it. "He would have told me, Julie. You've got it wrong."

"Why don't you get out of my car." She pulled over to the curb.

"Thanks for the ride," I said.

I wanted to talk to my father, but I was scared. Not scared of him, but scared of what I was going to find out. I didn't want to just say to him, *Dad, is this true?* Because the answer might be short and deadly.

He couldn't have sold it. I didn't believe it. I remembered the walks he used to take with Joanne and me when we were little. We always started on Taylor Avenue and ended up near Bridge Street in the old part of town. As we walked Joanne and I counted stores and blocks. "Twenty blocks to a mile," my father said. A block with ten stores was a tenblock. Every tenblock we'd get a prize, a stick of gum or a nickel. After twenty blocks we stopped for ice cream.

In the old part of town, we walked past plain little houses with tarred roofs and wire fences painted white, with small gardens on the side and in the back, and grape arbors. My father would show us things. A dog in a yard, a cage with rabbits. Sometimes he'd show us an odd addition somebody had put on the side of their house. He liked the different things people did to their houses. "Every house is different," he said, "just like every person is different." My father always met people he knew, and they'd notice my sister and me, and we'd have to stand around and be polite and wait for the grown-ups to get done talking. Even though he didn't grow up here my father loved Clifton Heights. To sell the old apartment house, to invite in the developers, would mean bringing in thousands of people and cars and traffic jams. It meant destroying the old neighborhood. My father wouldn't do that. What Julie said couldn't be true.

But as it turned out, the only place that it wasn't true was in my head.

Sunday morning after breakfast, he asked me to wash the Cadillac. I was polishing the chrome when he came out to get something out of the glove compartment. "Dad," I said, "did you sell the apartment house?"

He looked at me through the glass. The curve of the windshield distorted his face, made it wider, flattened out his cheeks, made his whole face look like a rubber mask. "Yes," he said.

"You sold the apartment house?"

"Yes. Why?"

"You sold it?" I had to keep saying it. "I thought you were never going to sell that house. I thought you loved that place. You even told me once you'd like to retire there, so you could look at the river every day!"

"George, George, George. Slow down." He got out and shut the door. "The building was beginning to

179

cost me money. It needed a new roof."

"Nothing wrong with that roof. Just because it leaks a little. What's going to happen to those people in the house?"

"The boiler's shot, the windows are going to have to be replaced. The plumbing! I could go on. There was no future in that building. It's a money-eater."

"You sold it?"

"Yes."

"You didn't tell me. You never said a word. Why'd you keep it secret? I had to hear about it from Julie!"

"So when do I have to report to you? When do you report to me? You do what you want to do. You get a job, you stop working for me, you stay overnight with people. . . .That's okay. It's your life. But it works both ways, son."

Did my father sell the house because I wouldn't work for him? Crazy thought, but it crossed my mind. "What about the people in the house?" I said again. "What are they going to do? Where are they going to go? What about that snoopy old lady on the first floor? And Julie's parents?"

"They're going to have to move." He was solid and hard, like a block that I couldn't penetrate. "I'll help people as much as I can, but I have to think about my own family."

"Not me! You weren't thinking about me when you did this. You did it for money, Dad. They offered you a lot of money, and you couldn't turn it down."

"So, my money isn't yours?"

"I don't want it. I don't want your money. I don't need it. I can earn my own."

"Polishing furniture? My independent son. What are you making, minimum wage? And what happens

180

when you want to start out in a little business of your own? Where does the money come from? Aren't you going to turn to Pop then?"

"Is it possible you did this so you could have money for me? Is that what you're saying? That's terrible! It means what happens to those people is my fault."

"Don't be so self-centered. And don't be so sensitive, my son. How about your mother? Can I worry about her? And your sister. Can I worry about her? How about me? Can I worry about myself? Life isn't like television. People get old, they get tired, they can't work. They get sick. How long do you think your mother and me are going to work this way? Are you going to pay for my funeral? Or are you going to build me a box?"

I threw down the chamois, because in another second I was going to throw it at him. I didn't want to listen to his crap. He was just making excuses, making me feel sorry for him, and guilty. Guilty! Guilty for not thinking about my mother and my sister, not thinking about the family. Guilty because I didn't want to be a hairdresser. Guilty because I liked wood. Guilty because I wanted to do things my own way.

I didn't call Julie. What could I tell her that she didn't already know? My father had sold the building, sold out, and I didn't want to talk about it. Not to her.

"I don't want to live with my father anymore," I said to Rosemary on the phone.

"Why not?"

I told her about the apartment house. "He did it for money. He talks about the family and his old age, but who needs a million dollars? That's just greed. I never

181

thought my father was like that. I've lost my respect for him."

"You can always leave," she said.

For her, it was simple. She'd done it already. And in a way, her parents had helped her along by breaking up. She could leave one parent and go to the other. She could leave her mother and go to her father. But was I ready to leave home? "Where am I going to go?" I said.

"You could stay here for a few days."

I had to think about a lot more than a few days. I wasn't going to leave school, and I'd have to work. How much could I afford to pay for a place? What did it cost to rent a room? I asked Rosemary what they paid for their apartment and what I heard scared me. That was more money than I could make at Lydia's in two months.

"What about where you work?" Rosemary said. "You stayed there a couple nights, didn't you? Maybe she'll let you live there and you'll watch the place for her."

It was such a simple, fantastic idea. I had to call my boss at once. I didn't see how Lydia could say no.

"Are you sure this is something you want to do, George?" Lydia said. "You're mad at your parents now, but that's going to change. Everybody gets mad at their parents."

"This isn't going to change."

"I don't know. . . . When are you going to be eighteen?"

"In two months."

She leaned back. "Well, I was working and supporting myself when I was sixteen. Your parents may not like me for doing this. . . . "

"You're not doing it, I am. It's my decision. You said you were planning to hire someone to watch the place. Why not me?"

"Okay. I'd just as soon it was you. But don't feel you have to stay when things clear up at home."

"My passionate son," my mother said. She was in my room while I packed. Joanne sat on the bed, using Magic Markers to decorate her sneakers. My father looked in once, then walked away.

"Where're you going?" I said, but he didn't answer me.

I wanted him to say something, start the argument all over again. His silence was hard to take. It put it all on me. Here, he'd been so good to me all his life. What had he ever done that was bad? And what was I doing to him now? Disappointing him. Leaving him. Deserting him.

I packed two of everything: two pairs of pants, two shirts, two pairs of pajamas, two pairs of socks. One to wear and one to wash.

"Tell me again," my mother said. "Why are you moving out? What are we doing that's so wrong? We owned a building. We bought it twenty years ago and now we sold it. Buildings are bought and sold every day, a hundred times a day. That's business. Why do you want us to be different?"

"What about the people who live there? Don't you think about them at all?"

"You want the truth? Are you going to hate me if I tell you? Are you going to stop talking to me?"

"Mom. I'm still talking to you."

"I know you. I know once you get an idea, there's

no shaking it loose. But the truth is, there's the real world and there's the idea of the world. And you're not in the real world yet."

"I don't think you should go," Joanne said. "I think it's stupid. Tell him, Mom. Tell him how much he's going to miss us."

"I'm not going to Mars, Joanne."

"Yeah, you're going to be here every day after school for your munchies and to use my computer."

"Think again, George," my mother said. "We're going to miss you."

I laced my knapsack shut. "I just feel like I have to do it, Mom. It's not because I don't love you."

Downstairs, my father was drinking a cup of coffee in the kitchen. He shook hands with me, then his hand went to his pocket.

"No money, Dad."

"Oh. Oh, of course, I almost forgot. That's what this whole thing is about. My son, the bleeding heart."

"I didn't hear that, Dad."

"Well, then, I didn't say it."

Joanne had the last word. "I know why you're doing this, George. It's a big show for Mom and Dad's benefit. You're going to be back. You know you are."

Chapter 28

It was lonely living in the back of the store. There was nobody to ask me if I'd eaten, and when, and had I done my homework and showered and made an appointment with the dentist, and what time had I come in the night before. Now I had to think about all those things, and I wasn't as scrupulous and persistent as my mother was on my behalf. Which meant that I had to face the fact that I had good intentions, good instincts, good training, but all of it didn't always add up the way it should have.

A lot of mornings, I didn't have time to eat because I'd gone to sleep late, or because I'd been talking to Rosemary half the night. Not that, even with enough time, I could have made myself an elaborate breakfast or an elaborate anything. I had a two-burner electric hot plate and no refrigerator. I shopped every day, and sometimes I forgot, and didn't feel like going out again, so there'd be nothing to do but eat crackers or stale breakfast cereal.

Lydia had had outside lights and burglar alarms installed after the break-in, but still, there were long spooky nights. A lot of nights I'd lock myself in and settle down with my books and snacks and the radio on and the telephone where I could reach it. I was aware that I was safe, but I still listened. I heard the whine of trucks, or a car engine suddenly revving up, or mice scratching under the floors. Or was it a hungry, mutant giant rat gnawing through the wall to get to me? And with that thought, it would be like the first night again with the store broken into and the plastic yawning open, and me in the back with my feelers out and my eyes big as a cat's.

I had a lot of time to think. Sometimes I thought about Rosemary and Julie, how they were alike and how they were different. Both of them were doers. They didn't wait for things to happen. But Rosemary flashed, she burned. Julie was quiet, deeper, slower.

Me? I waited. Maybe that was my whole strategy in life. Waiting. Waiting for life to show me its direction. Waiting for something to happen — and something always did. And it was always a surprise, always something I didn't expect.

It was as if I were moving through life with my eyes squinted, half closed, and then something bumped me, nudged me. I'd see it as I ran into it — whatever it was, this thing, this moment, this something that was out there for me and right for me. That was how I'd met Julie. A *ping* in the back of the head with a miniature marshmallow. That was how I'd stumbled into working for Lydia. And it was how I'd met Rosemary.

A year ago, six months ago, I didn't know her. I'd had my life all figured out. All the pieces in place. George going in a totally different direction. It was George and Julie forever. We were going to college together. Eventually I'd go to work for my father, someday own the business. At some point, Julie would open a medical office and we'd get married and settle down here or in Englewood, or if we could afford it, North Park. And now everything had changed.

Julie and I were going our own ways. I was working, getting involved with wood and old furniture. Was that going to be my life? And Rosemary — she was in my life somehow, but I wasn't completely sure how. I didn't see us fitting neatly together. She was an artist. I was — at this point — a furniture stripper. Would I do it all my life? And where was my life going to be? Clifton Heights? New York City? Los Angeles? Someplace I hadn't even thought of yet?

The bus to school was roundabout, so I usually rode my bike. It meant an hour in the morning and an hour at night. It rained a lot that spring and even though I wore a slicker, I still got soaked. Sometimes I was out early enough to stop at the house, but more usually it was after school. As Joanne pointed out, I managed to stop home two or three times a week for one thing or another, mostly to shower or do laundry.

Since I had moved out, Joanne and I were nicer to each other. She'd make something to eat, or I would, usually fruit-and-ice-cream softies in the blender. Then we'd sit around and talk. Every time I got up to leave, the lazy part of me said, Stay. Stay home. What difference does it make?

And I'd remember when Julie and I had broken up,

how she had insisted we couldn't see each other. At the time I thought she was just being hard. But now I saw that when there were hard things to do, it was better to do them clean, once and for all.

"Telephone, George," Lydia said.

"Thanks," I said. It took a moment to strip off the rubber gloves.

"Hi, George."

"Julie?" We hadn't talked since the day I'd jumped out of her car.

"I'd like to talk to you. Can we meet?"

Was it the apartment house again? "What's it about, Julie? Something we can talk about over the phone?" Would you believe I'd ever say that to Julie?

"I'd rather see you in person," she said, and we agreed she'd meet me at Lydia's after work.

I was cleaning up when Julie walked in. I took a few minutes to show her around, show off a little, and maybe put off our talk. Her father's car was in the parking lot, but we walked over to a playground not far from Lydia's. It had been a warm day, but it was cooling off now. I zipped up my jacket. We sat on the swings and I waited for her to speak.

"I'm getting nervous about school," she said. "Am I really going to medical school? Sometimes I'm not even sure I'm interested in science."

"Decisions are hard," I said.

"You seem to have worked things out for yourself."

"For now," I said. I started talking about what I was doing and how someday I'd like to make fine furniture. I began to feel as if it were the old days when we talked about everything and never took a step without one another. And the thought crept in that she was here because she wanted to start again.

She swung and I swung along with her, going up and coming down, looking over at her, looking at the way her hair ran out behind as she rode forward and wrapped around her face as she went back. The swing, the two of us side by side, the hair in her face. . . . I imagined her reaching over and taking my hand.

George. Do you know what I'm thinking?

I have an idea, Julie, but why don't you tell me?

I want to get back together with you, George.

Had I been waiting for Julie all these months? Was Rosemary just an interlude? Couldn't waiting be a kind of doing? The way you waited when you wrestled. You always had the choice. Go after your opponent, take risks, and maybe get pinned fast, or wait for an opening, choose the moment — your moment.

I want to get back together with you, George.

When she said it, I'd be smiling. Everything I'd once dreamed of being handed to me. And then what? Would it be just the smile and no words? And not saying it, would I say everything? *No, Julie. Not you. Not anymore.*

"George. . . ." Julie brought the swing to a standstill. "I want to tell you something. I know what I said that day in the car was unfair, and I'm sorry. I was angry at your father. I shouldn't have blamed you."

"Is that what you came to tell me?"

"Yes. It's been bothering me. And then I heard you moved out of your parents' house and I started to think — was it because of what I said to you? You were always so close to your parents. I envied you your family. You never fought with them the way I did with mine. I hate to think I was the cause. . . ."

"Well, don't think it."

"My parents talk about you all the time." She looked at me with those gray, quiet eyes, then she touched me lightly on the shoulder. "Are we still friends?"

I reached over and kissed her cheek. That was my answer.

Chapter 29

One Saturday night in April, I had my first visitors in a while. Lydia had left at five. I was eating the crusts of the pizza we had shared for lunch when there was a rap on the door. Not just a knock. *Bang!* Like someone trying to break in. I went for the baseball bat. "Who's there?"

"George? It's us."

I flipped on the light. It was Troy and Chris. "I was just going to brain you guys with this bat."

"I told you not to fool around," Chris said to Troy. "You're always barging into places." She was wearing a leotard and sweatpants. They'd just come from a gymnastic meet in Englewood where Chris had competed.

"So where's the food?" Troy said. He threw himself into a chair.

"Take it easy," I said. "You're going to break that. . . . I thought we'd buy food when we pick up Rosemary." The four of us had gotten together in the city the week before and gone to a movie. Chris and Rosemary had liked each other right away. Troy and Rosemary, I wasn't so sure about. They weren't quite at swords' point, but they did a lot of fencing.

Troy made do with a box of stale popcorn. "I knew you'd try to starve us." When Rosemary called from the bus stop, we all went out to get her, and on the way back we bought chili beans, tacos, ice cream, and a Robert Redford pie. Really just chocolate pudding with whipped cream on a graham cracker crust. Then, at Lydia's, we put the food out on a worktable. We had bought paper plates and cups, but we'd forgotten spoons and forks. I had one of each. Rosemary and I shared the fork and Chris and Troy shared the spoon.

Afterward, we sat around and talked about this and that, summer and college and where we were going. Chris was sitting on Troy's lap. She had been offered a basketball scholarship at Maryland, and Miami was interested in her, too. "He," she said, bouncing on Troy, "wants me to go to Cortland State, so we'll be close."

"Close to what?" I said.

"Binghamton," Troy said. "I'm going up there after we graduate, and work with my father in his restaurant. I want to see what the restaurant business is like. I might move there permanently."

"Binghamton?" I said. "Seriously?"

"It's not the end of the world."

"I thought the way you did, too, George," Chris said. "Now I like it."

"If things work out for my father and me," Troy

said, "we'll enlarge the place, work a piano lounge into it."

"Troy'll play the piano," Chris said.

"Also wash dishes and sweep the floor," Troy said. "I'm going to learn the business, from my knees up. What about you, Big Rosie?"

"What about me, Troyless? I promised my mother I'd visit this summer. Other than that, I may be teaching dance in the park this summer."

"How about school?" I said to Troy. "The restaurant business? You belong in college."

"You sound like my mother, George. What about you and college? What are you doing here?"

"I'm not brilliant, like you."

"Oh, cut the crap. I'm too lazy for school. Four more years — I'd shoot myself. Besides, how would I pay for it? And don't tell me football scholarship. I'm not going to get myself crippled so I can make some big-shot alumni happy."

The thing with Troy and his father took me by surprise. I thought he hardly knew his father. I'd seen Mr. Bonner only once in all the years I'd known Troy. It had always been Troy and his mother, and now, suddenly, it was Troy and his father. I couldn't help thinking about my father and me, how close we used to be and how separate we were these days. Ever since I went to work for Lydia, things had gone downhill. It was strange the way things worked out. The things you thought would never change, changed. And things you never thought would happen, happened.

I never thought my father and I would quarrel or Julie and I would break up. I couldn't imagine a Rosemary. I never dreamed of Troy in business with his father. And I would have laughed six months ago if you'd told me I wasn't going to college. Maybe I shouldn't even be too sure about that.

Rosemary stayed after Troy and Chris left. Alone, we stood in the dark and kissed. I reached up and held her face. "Is there a place for me to stay over?" she said.

I nodded. There were blankets in a blanket box and a hired man's bed where Lydia put her little boy, Dante, down to sleep sometimes when she brought him over. But the hired man's bed was too short for Rosemary and barely big enough for me. "Let's try the cot together," I said.

"We'll never make it."

"I'll give it to you, and I'll sleep on the floor. . . . Want to borrow a pair of my pajamas?" I gave her the clean pair and she put them on. I was putting mine on, too, and looking at her. We got on the bed together.

Rosemary held my hand. "I like Chris. She's sweet."

"Great bod."

"True."

"You noticed, too?"

"You think girls don't? Troy seems obnoxious at first, but I like him. I want to hear him play sometime."

"He's good."

We lay there holding hands and talking. When I couldn't stand it anymore, I kissed her. "I never thought I'd get over Julie."

"But did you?"

"Didn't I? I never thought I'd find someone else I'd like as much."

"And did you?"

"Didn't I . . . ?" We kissed again. The kiss made me love her.

Later, when Rosemary was asleep, I pulled the mattress out of the hired man's bed and threw it on the floor next to the cot. It was dark. The light from the front sent long shadows through the door. I lay there and thought about Rosemary and Julie and me, and Rosemary. . . .

Rosemary, who had come to me like a spirit. A voice, a jumble of words, an idea, a name, strings of words, words strung together across the face of a computer — and now here she was, warm and breathing. I listened for her breath. She was on her side, her lips parted. Mouth breathing, but so quietly that I could hardly hear it. I leaned close. I could feel her heat.

Chapter 30

I turned eighteen in May, May eleventh, to be exact. Eighteen years old. The big One-Eight. The end of high school in sight. We seniors were perched, as the principal told us, on the brink of the real world.

My mother was still talking about me coming home. "Your room is always there for you," she said. But going home was the wrong way to go. The wrong direction. "I moved out," I said to Rosemary, "and now I don't know if I'm ever going to go back."

The coolness between my father and me still bothered me. We talked, we were polite, but the old closeness was gone. Was this the way it was going to be from now on? Was that what growing up meant? With my mother, it was different. She was always sending me off with food or bringing care packages over to Lydia's. It was as if she were saying, I'm not so crazy about what you're doing, either, but you have your own life and I still love you.

From my father, though, I didn't feel anything but disapproval. He didn't like anything I was doing. And I couldn't forget how he'd sold the apartment house. There was a deep rift between us. So it was a surprise when he called and asked me what I wanted for my birthday.

"Probably nothing."

"You're only eighteen once. What's your wish?"

Yes, fairy godfather. What had Julie said? The property went for a million bucks? I'd never asked my father the details. I couldn't even think about that much money. Or maybe I didn't want to think about it, because it messed up my idea of myself and our family. We were ordinary people. What we had, we had because my parents had worked hard for it. Wasn't that what they told me all the time I was growing up?

"What's the silence mean?" my father said. "You don't want anything? Okay, I was going to buy you a Ferrari."

"Oh, God."

"Don't get on your high horse, my son. It's just a little joke. Your mother and I want to do something for your birthday."

"It's just another day, Dad."

"Maybe to you, but not to us."

He was snappy with me, but I thought I heard disappointment in his voice. I felt I was letting him down again. "If you want to, you can get me some wood-working tools," I said.

"You're going to have to tell me what. I don't know about your tools. I know scissors and combs."

"A set of wood chisels would be nice."

197

"Wood chisels!" my mother said. She was on the extension. "Is that a celebration? You can get tools anytime. I think we should have a party."

"A birthday party, Mom? I stopped having birthday parties when I was fourteen."

"Just a party in the family."

"Does that mean my girlfriend can't come?"

"You mean the one from New York?" my father said.

"Yes, Rosemary."

"Of course, you should bring her," my mother said.

There were six of us for the party. Joanne had invited her friend Ernie Paik. I got to choose where we ate, and Joanne and Ernie weren't too thrilled about my choice. It was an Indian restaurant where I'd eaten lunch once with Lydia. It had just opened. It was a little place, a storefront restaurant, with a few tables and chairs, and plants in the window. I thought it would be a nice place to go, and also give the family that ran it a few customers.

My parents only went to Angelo's or the Country Kitchen. At the Country Kitchen, they met their golfing pals. At Angelo's, it was the mayor and all the village big shots. From the outside Angelo's could have been a funeral home the way it was bricked up, with a solid door that didn't invite you in. Inside, though, it was like a private club, all plush and quiet, and white tablecloths and pink carnations, and Mrs. Angelo was always there to say something pleasant.

When we got to the Indian restaurant the family that ran the place was sitting in back, and they all jumped up when we came in. One of them pushed two tables together for us by the window. Someone else brought us water and extra chairs, and they were ready to serve us.

My father looked around as if I'd brought him to a lemonade stand. He treated his chair like it was an orange crate, and then he put a folded napkin under the leg of the table to stop it from rocking. "George took us on a picnic," he said to Rosemary.

The menu was a novelty for everyone but Rosemary, who'd been to Indian restaurants with her father. Joanne was polite and didn't say anything, but Ernie kept asking which word meant hamburger and fries. He knew he was being funny, but still, I was relieved when the fried chicken came and they liked it. Everybody thought the puffy bread, the poori, was great.

All through the dinner, I was aware of my father at the other end of the table sitting between Rosemary and my mother. I'd catch my father looking at me sometimes, giving me a cool look, as if he was trying to figure out who I was exactly. If our eyes met, he'd turn to Rosemary or my mother. I had the sense that he was nervous, too, but not as much as I was. I could hardly eat.

You shouldn't have left home. That's what my father sitting at the other end of the table seemed to be saying to me. And in my head I fought back. *Dad, did you stay home with your family? No, you told me yourself, you left when you were seventeen and went into the Navy. Your father didn't want you to do that. Do you always do what's right? You sit there above everyone else, making judgments, but you make mistakes. If that house belonged to me I wouldn't have sold it. Not for a million bucks. Not in a million years.*

Over dessert my mother raised her water glass and

toasted my birthday. "To my son, George." Everybody drank their water and she came around behind me and put her arms around me. "Say something, Leonard," she said to my father. "Your son is eighteen years old."

My father had a stingy little smile on his face as he looked around the table. "This is really nice," he said, and then he paused, as if he didn't know what to say next. "To my son, George, who is in charge of his life now."

The same thing I'd been thinking, but it had a different quality coming from my father. Was he being sarcastic? Was he telling me that I was cut off from my family? That this was the way it was going to be from now on? I got so upset it was hard for me to even look at him.

"Happy birthday, brother." Joanne reached over and smacked me on the back.

"Eighteen," Ernie said, shaking his head. "I'm not looking forward to eighteen. Maybe if you could stay eighteen forever."

"God forbid," my father said. Everyone laughed, and then my father called for the check.

Outside, Joanne said, "Who wants ice cream?" The spicy food had made everyone thirsty, and they all went across the street. I lagged behind, waiting for my father.

I felt I had to say something to him. *Thanks for the birthday party. Dad, you did the right thing, you gave me the party, you toasted me, you smiled. But you still don't like what I'm doing. And you still haven't said one real thing to me.*

And then we'd have a fight.

My father came out of the restaurant. He looked tired. "Where's everybody?"

"They went over for ice cream. You want some? I'll get it for you."

He patted his belly. "I don't need it. How about you? You need some money?" He started pulling out his wallet. "I remember you always liked mint chip ice cream the best, the stuff that tastes like chewing gum."

"Dad. . . ." He had money in his hand. "Dad. . . ."

Dad, let's talk. It's not money I want from you. You did something I don't like and never will, but you're still my father. And I did something you didn't want me to do, but I'm still your son.

"Dad, is there anything you want to tell me?"

"You mean words of wisdom?" He buttoned his jacket, then brushed a piece of lint off the sleeve. "What could I tell you?"

The others were beginning to come back. And I thought, he's too stiff to say anything real and I'm too dumb. It was too late, anyway. I couldn't talk in front of everyone. I saw Rosemary and started across the street to meet her.

"George . . ." my father said. I turned. He was standing there, holding out the money. "You forgot this."

I was in the middle of the street. There was no traffic, and I could have walked a long way in either direction. And I thought, if I just start walking, I might never see him again.

"Buy yourself something," he said. "It's your birthday money. You'll never be eighteen again."

"I don't want it," I said. "No money. I don't want money."

"What do you want then?"

Could I tell him? I wanted us to be the way we used to be — no speeches, no ceremonies, no money, no secret thoughts, no holding back, no holding each other at arm's length. I walked toward him. Was I going to wait for him to make the first move? Wait and wait and wait, and wait forever? Forever polite strangers? He at one end of the table and me at the other.

"Dad. . . ." I put my arms around him. He felt as movable as a mountain, but I hugged him.

"What's that for?" he said.

"I love you, Dad."

"Well," he said. "Well. You've got some way of showing it." But he put his arm around my shoulders and he kept it there all the way back to the car.

About the Author

Harry Mazer's sensitive and humorous novels have made him one of today's most popular writers for young adults. His many books include: *When the Phone Rang; The Last Mission; The War on Villa Street;* and *I Love You, Stupid!*, all of which were named Best Books for Young Adults by the American Library Association. He is co-author with his wife, Norma Fox Mazer, of *The Solid Gold Kid* (also an ALA Best Book for Young Adults) and has recently published *Hey, Kid! Does She Love Me?*

Harry Mazer lives with his wife in the Pompey Hills outside of Syracuse, New York.